D0924820

# CONTENTS

# THE WORLD'S 100 BEST SHORT STORIES

## THE BOY PENROD

### By Booth Tarkington

### Chapter I

#### A BOY AND HIS DOG

Penrod sat morosely upon the back fence and gazed with envy at Duke, his wistful dog.

A bitter soul dominated the various curved and angular surfaces known by a careless world as the face of Penrod Schofield. Except in solitude, that face was almost always cryptic and emotionless; for Penrod had come into his twelfth year wearing an expression carefully trained to be inscrutable. Since the world was sure to misunderstand everything, mere defensive instinct prompted him to give it as little as possible to lay hold upon. Nothing is more impenetrable than the face of a boy who has learned this, and Penrod's was habitually as fathomless as the depth of his hatred this morning for the literary activities of Mrs. Lora Rewbush—an almost universally respected fellow citizen, a lady of charitable and poetic inclinations, and one of his own mother's most intimate friends.

Mrs. Lora Rewbush had written something which she

(From "Penrod," by Booth Tarkington; copyright, 1914, by Doubleday-Page & Co.)

called "The Children's Pageant of the Table Round,"
and it was to be performed in public that very afternoon at the Women's Arts and Guild Hall for the
benefit of the Colored Infants' Betterment Society.
And if any flavor of sweetness remained in the nature
of Penrod Schofield after the dismal trials of the school-
week just past, that problematic, infinitesimal remnant
was made pungent acid by the imminence of his destiny
to form a prominent feature of the spectacle, and to
declaim the loathsome sentiments of a character named
upon the program the Child Sir Lancelot.

After each rehearsal he had plotted escape, and only
ten days earlier there had been a glimmer of light: Mrs.
Lora Rewbush caught a very bad cold, and it was hoped
it might develop into pneumonia; but she recovered so
quickly that not even a rehearsal of the Children's
Pageant was postponed. Darkness closed in. Penrod
had rather vaguely debated plans for a self-mutilation
such as would make his appearance as the Child Sir
Lancelot inexpedient on public grounds; it was a heroic
and attractive thought, but the results of some extremely sketchy preliminary experiments caused him to
abandon it.

There was no escape; and at last his hour was hard
upon him. Therefore he brooded on the fence and
gazed with envy at his wistful Duke.

The dog's name was undescriptive of his person,
which was obviously the result of a singular series of
mésalliances. He wore a grizzled mustache and in-
definite whiskers; he was small and shabby, and looked
like an old postman. Penrod envied Duke because he
was sure Duke would never be compelled to be a Child
Sir Lancelot. He thought a dog free and unshackled

to go or come as the wind listeth. Penrod forgot the life he led Duke.

There was a long soliloquy upon the fence, a plaintive monolog without words: the boy's thoughts were adjectives, but they were expressed by a running film of pictures in his mind's eye, morbidly prophetic of the hideosities before him. Finally he spoke aloud, with such spleen that Duke rose from his haunches and lifted one ear in keen anxiety.

> " 'I hight Sir Lancelot du Lake, the Child,
>  Gentul-hearted, meek, and mild.
>  What tho I'm *but* a littul child,
>  Gentul-hearted, meek, and——' *Oof!*"

All of this except "oof" was a quotation from the Child Sir Lancelot, as conceived by Mrs. Lora Rewbush. Choking upon it, Penrod slid down from the fence, and with slow and thoughtful steps entered a one-storied wing of the stable, consisting of a single apartment, floored with cement and used as a storeroom for broken bric-à-brac, old paint-buckets, decayed garden-hose, worn-out carpets, dead furniture, and other condemned odds and ends not yet considered hopeless enough to be given away.

In one corner stood a large box, a part of the building itself: it was eight feet high and open at the top, and it had been constructed as a sawdust magazine from which was drawn material for the horse's bed in a stall on the other side of the partition. The big box, so high and towerlike, so commodious, so suggestive, had ceased to fulfil its legitimate function; tho, providentially, it had been at least half full of sawdust when the horse died. Two years had gone by since that passing; an interregnum in transportation during which Penrod's father was "thinking" (he explained sometimes) of an automobile. Meanwhile, the gifted and generous sawdust-box had served brilliantly in war and peace: it was Penrod's stronghold.

There was a partially defaced sign upon the front wall of the box; the donjon-keep had known mercantile impulses:

> The O. K. RaBiT CO.
> PENROD ScHoFiELD AND CO.
> iNQuiRE FOR PRicEs

This was a venture of the preceding vacation, and had netted, at one time, an accrued and owed profit of $1.38. Prospects had been brightest on the very eve of cataclysm. The storeroom was locked and guarded, but twenty-seven rabbits and Belgian hares, old and young, had perished here on a single night—through no human agency, but in a foray of cats, the besiegers treacherously tunnelling up through the sawdust from the small aperture which opened into the stall beyond the partition. Commerce has its martyrs.

Penrod climbed upon a barrel, stood on tiptoe, grasped the rim of the box; then, using a knot-hole as a stirrup, threw one leg over the top, drew himself up, and dropped within. Standing upon the packed sawdust, he was just tall enough to see over the top.

Duke had not followed him into the storeroom, but remained near the open doorway in a concave and pessimistic attitude. Penrod felt in a dark corner of the box and laid hands upon a simple apparatus consisting of an old bushel-basket with a few yards of clothes-line tied to each of its handles. He passed the end of the lines over a big spool, which revolved upon an axle of wire suspended from a beam overhead, and, with the aid of this improvised pulley, lowered the empty basket

until it came to rest in an upright position upon the
floor of the storeroom at the foot of the sawdust-box.

"Eleva-ter!" shouted Penrod. "Ting-ting!"

Duke, old and intelligently apprehensive, approached
slowly, in a semicircular manner, deprecatingly, but
with courtesy. He pawed the basket delicately; then,
as if that were all his master had expected of him,
uttered one bright bark, sat down, and looked up
triumphantly. His hypocrisy was shallow: many a
horrible quarter of an hour had taught him his duty in
this matter.

"El-e-*vay*-ter!" shouted Penrod sternly. "You want
me to come down there *to* you?"

Duke looked suddenly haggard. He pawed the basket
feebly again and, upon another outburst from on high,
prostrated himself flat. Again threatened, he gave a
superb impersonation of a worm.

"You get in that el-e-vAy-ter!"

Reckless with despair, Duke jumped into the basket,
landing in a dishevelled posture, which he did not alter
until he had been drawn up and poured out upon the
floor of sawdust with the box. There, shuddering, he
lay in doughnut shape and presently slumbered.

It was dark in the box, a condition that might have
been remedied by sliding back a small wooden panel on
runners, which would have let in ample light from the
alley; but Penrod Schofield had more interesting means
of illumination. He knelt, and from a former soap-box,
in a corner, took a lantern without a chimney, and a
large oil-can, the leak in the latter being so nearly
imperceptible that its banishment from household use
had seemed to Penrod as inexplicable as it was provi-
dential.

He shook the lantern near his ear: nothing splashed;

there was no sound but a dry clinking. But there was
plenty of kerosene in the can; and he filled the lantern,
striking a match to illumine the operation. Then he lit
the lantern and hung it upon a nail against the wall.
The sawdust floor was slightly impregnated with oil,
and the open flame quivered in suggestive proximity to
the side of the box; however, some rather deep char-
ring of the plank against which the lantern hung offered
evidence that the arrangement was by no means a new
one, and indicated at least a possibility of no fatality
occurring this time.

Next, Penrod turned up the surface of the sawdust
in another corner of the floor, and drew forth a cigar-
box in which were half a dozen cigarets, made of
hayseed and thick brown wrapping paper, a lead-pencil,
an eraser, and a small note-book, the cover of which
was labelled in his own handwriting:

"English Grammar. Penrod Schofield.   Room 6,
Ward School Nomber Seventh."

The first page of this book was purely academic; but
the study of English undefiled terminated with a slight
jar at the top of the second: "Nor must an adverb be
used to modif——"

Immediately followed:

"HARoLD RAMoREZ THE RoADAGENT
OR WiLD LiFE AMoNG THE
ROCKY MTS."

And the subsequent entries in the book appeared to
have little concern with Room 6, Ward School Nomber
Seventh.

## Chapter II

### ROMANCE

The author of "Harold Ramorez," etc., lit one of the hayseed cigarets, seated himself comfortably, with his back against the wall and his right shoulder just under the lantern, elevated his knees to support the note-book, turned to a blank page, and wrote, slowly and earnestly:

## "CHAPITER THE SIXTH"

He took a knife from his pocket, and, broodingly, his eyes upon the inward embryos of vision, sharpened his pencil. After that, he extended a foot and medi-tatively rubbed Duke's back with the side of his shoe. Creation, with Penrod, did not leap, full-armed, from the brain; but finally he began to produce. He wrote very slowly at first, and then with increasing rapidity; faster and faster, gathering momentum and growing more and more fevered as he sped, till at last the true fire came, without which no lamp of real literature may be made to burn.

Mr. Wilson reched for his gun but our hero had him covred and soon said Well I guess you don't come any of that on me my friend.
Well what makes you so sure about it sneered the other bitting his lip so savageley that the blood ran. You are nothing but a common Roadagent any way and I do not propose to be bafled by such, Ramorez laughed at this and kep Mr. Wilson covred by his ottomatick
Soon the two men were struggling together in the deathroes but soon Mr. Wilson got him bound and gaged his mouth and went away for awhile leavin our hero, it was dark and he writhd at his bonds writhing on the floor wile the rats came out of their holes and bit him and vernim got all over him from the floor of that helish spot but soon he manged to push the gag out of his mouth with the end of his tcungeu and got all his bonds off

Soon Mr Wilson came back to tant him with his helpless condition flowed by his gang of detectives and they said Oh look at Ramorez sneering at his plight and tanted him with his helpless condition because Ramorez had put the bonds back sos he would look the same but could throw them off him when he wanted to. Just look at him now sneered they. To hear him talk you would thought he was hot stuff and they said Look at him now, him that was going to do so much. Oh I would not like to be in his fix

Soon Harold got mad at this and jumped up with blasing eyes throwin off his bonds like they were air Ha Ha sneered he I guess you better not talk so much next time. Soon there flowed another awful struggle and siezin his ottomatick back from Mr Wilson he shot two of the detectives through the heart Bing Bing went the ottomatick and two more went to meet their Maker only two detectives left now and so he stabbed one and the scondrel went to meet his Maker for now our hero was fighting for his very life. It was dark in there now for night had falen and a terrible view met the eye Blood was just all over everything and the rats were eatin the dead men.

Soon our hero manged to get his back to the wall for he was fighting for his very life now and shot Mr Wilson through the abodmen Oh said Mr Wilson you—— —— ——(*The dashes are Penrod's.*)

Mr Wilson stagerd back vile oaths soilin his lips for he was in pain Why you——— ——you sneered he I will get you yet —— ——you Harold Ramorez

The remainin scondrel had an ax which he came near our heros head with but missed him and ramand stuck in the wall Our heros ammunition was exhausted what was he to do so, the remanin scondrel would soon get his ax lose so our hero sprung forward and bit him till his teeth met in the flech for now our hero was fighting for his very life. At this the remainin scondrel also cursed and swore vile oaths. Oh sneered he—— —— ——you Harold Ramorez what did you bite me for Yes sneered Mr Wilson also and he has shot me in the abodmen too the——

Soon they were both cursin and reviln him together Why you——— —— —— ——sneered they what did you want to injure us for—you Harold Ramorez you have not got any sence and you think you are so much but you are no better than anybody else and you are a——— —— —— —— ——

Soon our hero could stand this no longer. If you could learn to act like gentlmen said he I would not do any more to you now and your low vile exppresions have not got any effect on me only to injure your own self when you go to meet your Maker Oh I guess you have had enogh for one day and I think you have learned a lesson and will not soon atemp to beard Harold Ramorez again so with a tantig laugh he cooly lit a cigarrete and takin the keys of the cell from Mr Wilson poket went on out

Soon Mr Wilson and the wonded detective manged to bind up their wonds and got up off the floor—— ——it I will have that dasstads life now sneered they if we have to swing for it—— —— —— ——him he shall not eccape us again the low down

### Chapter seventh

A mule train of heavily laden burros laden with gold from the mines was to be seen wondering among the highest clifts and gorgs of the Rocky Mts and a tall man with a long silken mustash and a cartidge belt could be heard cursin vile oaths because he well knew this was the lair of Harold Ramorez Why—— —— ——you you—— —— —— —— mules you sneered he because the poor mules were not able to go any quicker——you I will show you Why—— —— —— —— ——it sneered he his oaths growing viler and viler I will whip you—— —— —— —— —— —— ——you sos you will not be able to walk for a week—— ——you you mean old—— —— —— —— —— —— —— ——mules you

Scarcly had the vile words left his lips when——

*"Penrod!"*

It was his mother's voice, calling from the back porch.

Simultaneously, the noon whistle began to blow, far and near; and the romancer in the sawdust-box, summoned prosaically from steep mountain passes above the clouds, paused with stubby pencil halfway from lip to knee. His eyes were shining: there was a rapt sweetness in his gaze. As he wrote, his burden had grown lighter; thoughts of Mrs. Lora Rewbush had almost left him; and in particular as he recounted (even by the chaste dash) the annoyed expressions of Mr. Wilson, the wounded detective, and the silken mustached mule-driver, he had felt mysteriously relieved concerning the Child Sir Lancelot. Altogether he looked a better and a brighter boy.

"Pen-*rod!*"

The rapt look faded slowly. He sighed, but moved not.

"Penrod! We're having lunch early just on your account, so you'll have plenty of time to be dressed for the pageant. Hurry!"

There was silence in Penrod's aerie.

*"Pen-*rod!*"*

Mrs. Schofield's voice sounded nearer, indicating a threatened approach. Penrod bestirred himself: he blew out the lantern, and shouted plaintively:

"Well, ain't I coming fast's I can?"

"Do hurry," returned the voice, withdrawing; and the kitchen door could be heard to close.

Languidly, Penrod proceeded to set his house in order.

Replacing his manuscript and pencil in the cigar-box, he carefully buried the box in the sawdust, put the lantern and oil-can back in the soap-box, adjusted the elevator for the reception of Duke, and, in no uncertain tone, invited the devoted animal to enter.

Duke stretched himself amiably, affecting not to hear; and when this pretense became so obvious that even a dog could keep it up no longer, sat down in a corner, facing it, his back to his master, and his head perpendicular, nose upward, supported by the convergence of the two walls. This, from a dog, is the last word, the *comble* of the immutable. Penrod commanded, stormed, tried gentleness; persuaded with honeyed words and pictured rewards. Duke's eyes looked backward; otherwise he moved not. Time elapsed. Penrod stooped to flattery, finally to insincere caresses; then, losing patience, spouted sudden threats. Duke remained immovable, frozen fast to his great gesture of implacable despair.

A footstep sounded on the threshold of the store-room.

"Penrod, come down from that box this instant!"

"Ma'am?"

"Are you up in that sawdust-box again?" As Mrs. Schofield had just heard her son's voice issue from the box, and also, as she knew he was there anyhow, her question must have been put for oratorical purposes only. "Because if you are," she continued promptly, "I'm going to ask your papa not to let you play there any——"

Penrod's forehead, his eyes, the tops of his ears, and most of his hair, became visible to her at the top of the box. "I ain't 'playing!'" he said indignantly.

"Well, what *are* you doing?"

"Just coming down," he replied, in a grieved but patient tone.

"Then why don't you *come?*"

"I got Duke here. I got to get him *down*, haven't I? You don't suppose I want to leave a poor dog in here to starve, do you?"

"Well, hand him down over the side to me. Let me——"

"I'll get him down all right," said Penrod. "I got him up here, and I guess I can get him down!"

"Well then, *do* it!"

"I will if you'll let me alone. If you'll go on back to the house I promise to be there inside of two minutes Honest!"

He put extreme urgency into this, and his mother turned toward the house. "If you're not there in two minutes——"

"I will be!"

After her departure, Penrod expended some finalities of eloquence upon Duke, then disgustedly gathered him up in his arms, dumped him into the basket and, shouting sternly, "All in for the ground floor—step back there, madam—all ready, Jim!" lowered dog and basket to the floor of the storeroom. Duke sprang out in tumultuous relief, and bestowed frantic affection upon his master as the latter slid down from the box.

Penrod dusted himself sketchily, experiencing a sense of satisfaction, dulled by the overhanging afternoon, perhaps, but perceptible: he had the feeling of one who has been true to a cause. The operation of the elevator was unsinful and, save for the shock to Duke's nervous system, it was harmless; but Penrod could not possibly have brought himself to exhibit it in the presence of his mother or any other grown person in the world. The reasons for secrecy were undefined; at least, Penrod did not define them.

## Chapter III

### THE COSTUME

After lunch his mother and his sister Margaret, a pretty girl of nineteen, dressed him for the sacrifice. They stood him near his mother's bedroom window and did what they would to him.

During the earlier anguishes of the process he was mute, exceeding the pathos of the stricken calf in the shambles; but a student of eyes might have perceived in his soul the premonitory symptoms of a sinister uprising. At a rehearsal (in citizens' clothes) attended by mothers and grown-up sisters, Mrs. Lora Rewbush had announced that she wished the costuming to be "as medieval and artistic as possible." Otherwise, and as to details, she said, she would leave the costumes entirely to the good taste of the children's parents. Mrs. Schofield and Margaret were no archeologists, but they knew that their taste was as good as that of other mothers and sisters concerned; so with perfect confidence they had planned and executed a costume for

Penrod; and the only misgiving they felt was connected with the tractability of the Child Sir Lancelot himself.

Stripped to his underwear, he had been made to wash himself vehemently; then they began by shrouding his legs in a pair of silk stockings, once blue but now mostly whitish. Upon Penrod they visibly surpassed mere ampleness; but they were long, and it required only a rather loose imagination to assume that they were tights.

The upper part of his body was next concealed from view by a garment so peculiar that its description becomes difficult. In 1886, Mrs. Schofield, then unmarried, had worn at her "coming-out party" a dress of vivid salmon silk which had been remodelled after her marriage to accord with various epochs of fashion until a final, unskilful campaign at a dye-house had left it in a condition certain to attract much attention to the wearer. Mrs. Schofield had considered giving it to Della, the cook; but had decided not to do so, because you never could tell how Della was going to take things, and cooks were scarce.

It may have been the word "medieval" (in Mrs. Lora Rewbush's rich phrase) which had inspired the idea for a last conspicuous usefulness; at all events, the bodice of that once salmon dress, somewhat modified and moderated, now took a position, for its farewell appearance in society, upon the back, breast, and arms of the Child Sir Lancelot.

The area thus costumed ceased at the waist, leaving a Jaeger-like and unmedieval gap thence to the tops of the stockings. The inventive genius of woman triumphantly bridged it, but in a manner which imposes upon history almost insuperable delicacies of narration. Penrod's father was an old-fashioned man: the twentieth century had failed to shake his faith in red flannel for cold weather; and it was while Mrs. Schofield was putting away her husband's winter underwear that she perceived how hopelessly one of the elder specimens had dwindled; and simultaneously she received the inspiration which resulted in a pair of trunks for the Child Sir Lancelot, and added an earnest bit of color, as well as a genuine touch of the Middle Ages, to his costume. Reversed, fore to aft, with the greater part of the legs cut off, and strips of silver braid covering the seams, this garment, she felt, was not traceable to its original source.

When it had been placed upon Penrod, the stockings were attached to it by a system of safety-pins, not very perceptible at a distance. Next, after being severely warned against stooping, Penrod got his feet into the slippers he wore to dancing-school—"patent-leather pumps" now decorated with large pink rosettes.

"If I can't stoop," he began, smolderingly, "I'd like to know how'm I goin' to kneel in the pag——"

"You must *manage!*" This, uttered through pins, was evidently thought to be sufficient.

They fastened some ruching about his slender neck, pinned ribbons at random all over him, and then Margaret thickly powdered his hair.

"Oh, yes, that's all right," she said, replying to a question put by her mother. "They always powdered their hair in Colonial times."

"It doesn't seem right to me—exactly," objected Mrs. Schofield, gently. "Sir Lancelot must have been ever so long before Colonial times."

"That doesn't matter," Margaret reassured her. "Nobody'll know the difference—Mrs. Lora Rewbush least of all. I don't think she knows a thing about it,

tho, of course, she does write splendidly and the
words of the pageant are just beautiful. Stand still,
Penrod!" (The author of "Harold Ramorez" had
moved convulsively.) "Besides, powdered hair's always
becoming. Look at him. You'd hardly know it was
Penrod!"

The pride and admiration with which she pronounced
this undeniable truth might have been thought tactless,
but Penrod, not analytical, found his spirits somewhat
elevated. No mirror was in his range of vision and,
tho he had submitted to cursory measurements of
his person a week earlier, he had no previous ac-
quaintance with the costume. He began to form a not
unpleasing mental picture of his appearance, something
somewhere between the portraits of George Washington and a vivid memory of Miss Julia Marlowe at a
matinée of "Twelfth Night."

He was additionally cheered by a sword which had
been borrowed from a neighbor, who was a Knight of
Pythias. Finally there was a mantle, an old golf cape
of Margaret's. Fluffy polka-dots of white cotton had
been sewed to it generously; also it was ornamented
with a large cross of red flannel, suggested by the picture of a Crusader in a newspaper advertisement. The
mantle was fastened to Penrod's shoulder (that is, to
the shoulder of Mrs. Schofield's ex-bodice) by means
of large safety-pins, and arranged to hang down behind
him, touching his heels, but obscuring nowise the glory
of his façade. Then, at last, he was allowed to step
before a mirror.

It was a full-length glass, and the worst immediately
happened. It might have been a little less violent, perhaps, if Penrod's expectations had not been so richly

and poetically idealized; but as things were, the revolt was volcanic.

Victor Hugo's account of the fight with the devil-fish, in "Toilers of the Sea," encourages a belief that, had Hugo lived and increased in power, he might have been equal to a proper recital of the half hour which followed Penrod's first sight of himself as the Child Sir Lancelot. But Mr. Wilson himself, dastard but eloquent foe of Harold Ramorez, could not have expressed, with all the vile dashes at his command, the sentiments which animated Penrod's bosom when the instantaneous and unalterable conviction descended upon him that he was intended by his loved ones to make a public spectacle of himself in his sister's stockings and part of an old dress of his mother's.

To him these familiar things were not disguised at all; there seemed no possibility that the whole world would not know them at a glance. The stockings were worse than the bodice. He had been assured that these could not be recognized but, seeing them in the mirror, he was sure that no human eye could fail at first glance to detect the difference between himself and the former purposes of these stockings. Fold, wrinkle, and void shrieked their history with a hundred tongues, invoking earthquake, eclipse, and blue ruin. The frantic youth's final submission was obtained only after a painful telephonic conversation between himself and his father, the latter having been called up and upon, by the exhausted Mrs. Schofield, to subjugate his offspring by wire.

The two ladies made all possible haste, after this, to deliver Penrod into the hands of Mrs. Lora Rewbush; nevertheless, they found opportunity to exchange earnest congratulations upon his not having recognized the humble but serviceable paternal garment now brilliant about the Lancelotish middle. Altogether, they felt that the costume was a success. Penrod looked like nothing ever remotely imagined by Sir Thomas Malory or Alfred Tennyson;—for that matter, he looked like nothing ever before seen on earth; but as Mrs. Schofield and Margaret took their places in the audience at the Women's Arts and Guild Hall, the anxiety they felt concerning Penrod's elocutionary and gesticular powers, so soon to be put to public test, was pleasantly tempered by their satisfaction that, owing to their efforts, his outward appearance would be a credit to the family.

## Chapter IV

### DESPERATION

The Child Sir Lancelot found himself in a large anteroom behind the stage—a room crowded with excited children, all about equally medieval and artistic. Penrod was less conspicuous than he thought himself, but he was so preoccupied with his own shame, steeling his nerves to meet the first inevitable taunting reference to his sister's stockings, that he failed to perceive there were others present in much of his own unmanned condition. Retiring to a corner, immediately upon his entrance, he managed to unfasten the mantle at the shoulders, and, drawing it round him, pinned it again at his throat so that it concealed the rest of his costume. This permitted a temporary relief, but increased his horror of the moment when, in pursuance of the action of the "pageant," the sheltering garment must be cast aside.

Some of the other child knights were also keeping their mantles close about them. A few of the envied opulent swung brilliant fabrics from their shoulders airily, showing off hired splendors from a professional costumer's stock, while one or two were insulting examples of parental indulgence, particularly little Maurice Levy, the Child Sir Galahad. This shrinking person went clamorously about, making it known everywhere that the best tailor in town had been dazzled by a great sum into constructing his costume. It consisted of blue velvet knickerbockers, a white satin waistcoat, and a beautifully cut little swallow-tailed coat with pearl buttons. The medieval and artistic triumph was completed by a mantle of yellow velvet, and little white boots, sporting gold tassels.

All this radiance paused in a brilliant career and addressed the Child Sir Lancelot, gathering an immediately formed semicircular audience of little girls. Woman was ever the trailer of magnificence.

"What *you* got on?" inquired Mr. Levy, after dispensing information. "What you got on under that ole golf cape?"

Penrod looked upon him coldly. At other times his questioner would have approached him with deference, even with apprehension. But to-day the Child Sir Galahad was somewhat intoxicated with the power of his own beauty.

"What *you* got on?" he repeated.

"Oh, nothin'," said Penrod, with an indifference assumed at great cost to his nervous system.

The elate Maurice was inspired to set up as a wit. "Then you're nakid!" he shouted exultantly. "Penrod Schofield says he hasn't got nothin' on under that ole golf cape! He's nakid! He's nakid!"

The indelicate little girls giggled delightedly, and a javelin pierced the inwards of Penrod when he saw that the Child Elaine, amber-curled and beautiful Marjorie Jones, lifted golden laughter to the horrid jest.

Other boys and girls came flocking to the uproar. "He's nakid, he's nakid!" shrieked the Child Sir Galahad. "Penrod Schofield's nakid! He's *na-a-a-kid!*"

"Hush, hush!" said Mrs. Lora Rewbush, pushing her way into the group. "Remember, we are all little knights and ladies to-day. Little knights and ladies of the Table Round would not make so much noise. Now children, we must begin to take our places on the stage. Is everybody here?"

Penrod made his escape under cover of this diversion: he slid behind Mrs. Lora Rewbush and being near a door, opened it unnoticed and went out quickly, closing it behind him. He found himself in a narrow and vacant hallway which led to a door marked "Janitor's Room."

Burning with outrage, heart-sick at the sweet, cold-blooded laughter of Marjorie Jones, Penrod rested his elbows upon a window-sill and speculated upon the effects of a leap from the second story. One of the reasons he gave it up was his desire to live on Maurice Levy's account: already he was forming educational plans for the Child Sir Galahad.

A stout man in blue overalls passed through the hallway muttering to himself petulantly. "I reckon they'll find that hall hot enough *now!*" he said, conveying to Penrod an impression that some too feminine women had sent him upon an unreasonable errand to the furnace. He went into the Janitor's Room and, emerging a moment later, minus the overalls, passed Penrod again with a bass rumble—"Dern 'em!" it

seemed he said—and made a gloomy exit by the door
at the upper end of the hallway.

The conglomerate and delicate rustle of a large, man-
nerly audience was heard as the janitor opened and
closed the door; and stage-fright seized the boy. The
orchestra began an overture, and, at that, Penrod,
trembling violently, tiptoed down the hall into the
Janitor's Room. It was a cul-de-sac: There was no
outlet save by the way he had come.

Despairingly he doffed his mantle and looked down
upon himself for a last sickening assurance that the
stockings were as obviously and disgracefully Margaret's as they had seemed in the mirror at home. For
a moment he was encouraged: perhaps he was no worse
than some of the other boys. Then he noticed that a
safety-pin had opened; one of those connecting the
stockings with his trunks. He sat down to fasten it
and his eye fell for the first time with particular attention upon the trunks. Until this instant he had been
preoccupied with the stockings.

Slowly recognition dawned in his eyes.

The Schofields' house stood on a corner at the inter-
section of two main-traveled streets; the fence was
low, and the publicity obtained by the washable portion
of the family apparel, on Mondays, had often been
painful to Penrod; for boys have a peculiar sensitive-
ness in these matters. A plain, matter-of-fact washer-
woman, employed by Mrs. Schofield, never left anything to the imagination of the passerby; and of all her
calm display the scarlet flaunting of his father's winter
wear had most abashed Penrod. One day Marjorie
Jones, all gold and starch, had passed when the dreadful
things were on the line: Penrod had hidden himself,

shuddering. The whole town, he was convinced, knew these garments intimately and derisively.

And now, as he sat in the janitor's chair, the horrible and paralyzing recognition came. He had not an instant's doubt that every fellow actor, as well as every soul in the audience, would recognize what his mother and sister had put upon him. For as the awful truth became plain to himself it seemed blazoned to the world; and far, far louder than the stockings, the trunks did fairly bellow the grisly secret: *whose* they were and WHAT they were!

Most people have suffered in a dream the experience of finding themselves very inadequately clad in the midst of a crowd of well-dressed people, and such dreamers' sensations are comparable to Penrod's, tho faintly, because Penrod was awake and in much too full possession of the most active capacities for anguish.

A human male whose dress has been damaged, or reveals some vital lack, suffers from a hideous and shameful loneliness which makes every second absolutely unbearable until he is again as others of his sex and species; and there is no act or sin whatever too desperate for him in his struggle to attain that condition. Also, there is absolutely no embarrassment possible to a woman which is comparable to that of a man under corresponding circumstances; and in this a boy is a man. Gazing upon the ghastly trunks, the stricken Penrod felt that he was a degree worse than nude; and a great horror of himself filled his soul.

"Penrod Schofield!"

The door into the hallway opened, and a voice demanded him. He could not be seen from the hallway, but the hue and the cry was up; and he knew he must be taken. It was only a question of seconds. He huddled in his chair.

"Penrod Schofield!" cried Mrs. Lora Rewbush angrily.

The distracted boy rose and, as he did so, a long pin sank deep into his back. He extracted it frenziedly, which brought to his ears a protracted and sonorous ripping, too easily located by a final gesture of horror.

"Penrod Schofield!" Mrs. Lora Rewbush had come out into the hallway.

And now, in this extremity, when all seemed lost indeed, particularly including honor, the dilating eye of the outlaw fell upon the blue overalls which the janitor had left hanging upon a peg.

Inspiration and action were almost simultaneous.

## Chapter V

### THE PAGEANT OF THE TABLE ROUND

"Penrod!" Mrs. Lora Rewbush stood in the doorway, indignantly gazing upon a Child Sir Lancelot mantled to the heels. "Do you know that you have kept an audience of five hundred people waiting for ten minutes?" She, also, detained the five hundred while she spake further.

"Well," said Penrod contentedly, as he followed her toward the buzzing stage, "I was just sitting there thinking."

Two minutes later the curtain rose on a medieval castle hall richly done in the new stage-craft made in Germany and consisting of pink and blue cheese-cloth. The Child King Arthur and the Child Queen Guinevere were disclosed upon thrones, with the Child

Elaine and many other celebrities in attendance; while about fifteen Child Knights were seated at a dining-room table round, which was covered with a large Oriental rug, and displayed (for the knights' refreshment) a banquet service of silver loving-cups and trophies, borrowed from the Country Club and some local automobile manufacturers.

In addition to this splendor, potted plants and palms have seldom been more lavishly used in any castle on the stage or off. The footlights were aided by a "spot-light" from the rear of the hall; and the children were revealed in a blaze of glory.

A hushed, multitudinous "O-*oh*" of admiration came from the decorous and delighted audience. Then the children sang feebly:

> "Chuldrun of the Tabul Round,
>    Lit-tul knights and ladies we,
> Let our voy-siz all resound
>    Faith and hope and charitee!"

The Child King Arthur rose, extended his scepter with the decisive gesture of a semaphore, and spake:

> "Each littul knight and lady born
> Has noble deeds *to* perform
> In *thee* child-world of shivullree,
> No matter how small his share may be.
> Let each advance and tell in turn
> What claim has each to knighthood earn."

The Child Sir Mordred, the villain of this piece, rose in his place at the table round, and piped the only lines ever written by Mrs. Lora Rewbush which Penrod Schofield could have pronounced without loathing. Georgie Bassett, a really angelic boy, had been selected for the rôle of Mordred. His perfect conduct had earned for him the sardonic sobriquet, "The Little Gentleman," among his boy acquaintances.

(Naturally he had no friends.)  Hence the other boys
supposed that he had been selected for the wicked
Mordred as a reward of virtue.  He declaimed serenely:

> "I hight Sir Mordred the Child, and I teach
> Lessons of selfishest evil, and reach
> Out into darkness.  Thoughtless, unkind,
> And ruthless is Mordred, and unrefined."

The Child Mordred was properly rebuked and denied
the accolade, tho, like the others, he seemed to
have assumed the title already.  He made a plotter's
exit.  Whereupon Maurice Levy rose, bowed, announced that he highted the Child Sir Galahad, and
continued with perfect *sang-froid*:

> "I am the purest of the pure.
> I have but kindest thoughts each day.
> I give my riches to the poor,
> And follow in the Master's way."

This elicited tokens of approval from the Child
King Arthur, and he bade Maurice "stand forth" and
come near the throne, a command obeyed with the
easy grace of conscious merit.

It was Penrod's turn.  He stepped back from his
chair, the table between him and the audience, and
began in a high, breathless monotone:

> "I hight Sir Lancelot du Lake, the Child,
> Gentul-hearted, meek, and mild.
> What tho I'm *but* a littul child,
> Gentul-hartud, meek, and mild,
> I do my share tho but—tho but——"

Penrod paused and gulped.  The voice of Mrs. Lora
Rewbush was heard from the wings, prompting irri-
tably, and the Child Sir Lancelot repeated:

> "I do my share tho but—tho but a tot,
> I pray you knight Sir Lancelot!"

This also met the royal favor, and Penrod was bidden to join Sir Galahad at the throne. As he crossed the stage, Mrs. Schofield whispered to Margaret:

"That boy! He's unpinned his mantle and fixed it to cover his whole costume. After we worked so hard to make it becoming!"

"Never mind; he'll have to take the cape off in a minute," returned Margaret. She leaned forward suddenly, narrowing her eyes to see better. "What *is* that thing hanging about his left ankle?" she whispered uneasily. "How queer! He must have got tangled in something."

"Where?" asked Mrs. Schofield, in alarm.

"His left foot. It makes him stumble. Don't you see? It looks—it looks like an elephant's foot!"

The Child Sir Lancelot and the Child Sir Galahad clasped hands before their Child King. Penrod was conscious of a great uplift; in a moment he would have to throw aside his mantle, but even so he was protected and sheltered in the human garment of a man. His stage-fright had passed, for the audience was but an indistinguishable blur of darkness beyond the dazzling lights. His most repulsive speech (that in which he proclaimed himself a "tot") was over and done with; and now at last the small, moist hand of the Child Sir Galahad lay within his own. Craftily his brown fingers stole from Maurice's palm to the wrist. The two boys declaimed in concert:

"We are two chuldrun cf the Tabul Round
   Strewing kindness all a-round.
With love and good deeds striving ever for the best,
   May our littul efforts e'er be blest.
Two littul hearts we offer. See
United in love, faith, hope, and char—*Ow!*"

The conclusion of the duet was marred. The Child
Sir Galahad suddenly stiffened, and, uttering an irrepressible shriek of anguish, gave a brief exhibition of
the contortionist's art. (*"He's twistin' my wrist! Dern
you, leggo!"*)

The voice of Mrs. Lora Rewbush was again heard
from the wings; it sounded bloodthirsty. Penrod re-
leased his victim; and the Child King Arthur, somewhat disconcerted, extended his scepter and, with the
assistance of the enraged prompter, said:

> "Sweet child-friends of the Tabul Round,
> In brotherly love and kindness abound,
>     Sir Lancelot, you have spoken well,
>     Sir Galahad, too, as clear as bell.
> So now pray doff your mantles gay.
> You shall be knighted this very day."

And Penrod doffed his mantle.

Simultaneously, a thick and vasty gasp came from
the audience, as from five hundred bathers in a wholly
unexpected surf. This gasp was punctuated irregularly,
over the auditorium, by imperfectly subdued screams
both of dismay and incredulous joy, and by two dismal
shrieks. Altogether it was an extraordinary sound, a
sound never to be forgotten by any one who heard
it. It was almost as unforgettable as the sight which
caused it; the word "sight" being here used in its
vernacular sense, for Penrod, standing unmantled and
revealed in all the medieval and artistic glory of the
janitor's blue overalls, falls within its meaning.

The janitor was a heavy man, and his overalls,
upon Penrod, were merely oceanic. The boy was at
once swaddled and lost within their blue gulfs and
vast saggings; and the left leg, too hastily rolled
up, had descended with a distinctively elephantine

effect, as Margaret had observed. Certainly, the Child Sir Lancelot was at least a sight.

It is probable that a great many in that hall must have had, even then, a consciousness that they were looking on at History in the Making. A supreme act is recognizable at sight: it bears the birthmark of immortality. But Penrod, that marvellous boy, had begun to declaim, even with the gesture of flinging off his mantle for the accolade:

> "I first, the Child Sir Lancelot du Lake,
>   Will volunteer to knighthood take,
> And kneeling here before your throne
>   I vow to——"

He finished his speech unheard. The audience had recovered breath, but had lost self-control, and there ensued something later described by a participant as a sort of cultured riot.

The actors in the "pageant" were not so dumfounded by Penrod's costume as might have been expected. A few precocious geniuses perceived that the overalls were the Child Lancelot's own comment on maternal intentions; and these were profoundly impressed: they regarded him with the grisly admiration of young and ambitious criminals for a jailmate about to be distinguished by hanging. But most of the children simply took it to be the case (a little strange, but not startling) that Penrod's mother had dressed him like that—which is pathetic. They tried to go on with the "pageant."

They made a brief, manful effort. But the irrepressible outbursts from the audience bewildered them; every time Sir Lancelot du Lake the Child opened his mouth, the great, shadowy house fell into an

uproar, and the children into confusion. Strong women
and brave girls in the audience went out into the
lobby, shrieking and clinging to one another. Others
remained, rocking in their seats, helpless and spent.
The neighborhood of Mrs. Schofield and Margaret
became, tactfully, a desert. Friends of the author went
behind the scenes and encountered a hitherto unknown
phase of Mrs. Lora Rewbush; they said, afterward,
that she hardly seemed to know what she was doing.
She begged to be left alone somewhere with Penrod
Schofield, for just a little while.

They led her away.

## Chapter VI

### EVENING

The sun was setting behind the back fence (tho at
a considerable distance) as Penrod Schofield approached
that fence and looked thoughtfully up at the top of it,
apparently having in mind some purpose to climb up
and sit there. Debating this, he passed his fingers
gently up and down the backs of his legs; and then
something seemed to decide him not to sit anywhere.
He leaned against the fence, sighed profoundly, and
gazed at Duke, his wistful dog.

The sigh was reminiscent: episodes of simple pathos
were passing before his inward eye. About the most
painful was the vision of lovely Marjorie Jones, weeping with rage as the Child Sir Lancelot was dragged,
insatiate, from the prostrate and howling Child Sir
Galahad, after an onslaught delivered the precise instant the curtain began to fall upon the demoralized

"pageant." And then—oh, pangs! oh, woman!—she slapped at the ruffian's cheek, as he was led past her by a resentful janitor; and turning, flung her arms round the Child Sir Galahad's neck.

*"Penrod Schofield, don't you dare ever speak to me again as long as you live!"* Maurice's little white boots and gold tassels had done their work.

At home the late Child Sir Lancelot was consigned to a locked clothes-closet pending the arrival of his father. Mr. Schofield came and, shortly after, there was put into practise an old patriarchal custom. It is a custom of inconceivable antiquity: probably primordial, certainly prehistoric, but still in vogue in some remaining citadels of the ancient simplicities of the Republic.

And now, therefore, in the dusk, Penrod leaned against the fence and sighed.

His case is comparable to that of an adult who would have survived a similar experience. Looking back to the sawdust-box, fancy pictures this comparable adult a serious and inventive writer engaged in congenial literary activities in a private retreat. We see this period marked by the creation of some of the most virile passages of a Work dealing exclusively in red corpuscles and huge primal impulses. We see this thoughtful man dragged from his calm seclusion to a horrifying publicity; forced to adopt the stage and, himself a writer, compelled to exploit the repulsive sentiments of an author not only personally distasteful to him but whose whole method and school in *belles lettres* he despises.

We see him reduced by desperation and modesty to stealing a pair of overalls. We conceive him to have ruined, then, his own reputation, and to have utterly

disgraced his family; next, to have engaged in the
duello and to have been spurned by his lady-love,
thus lost to him (according to her own declaration)
forever.  Finally, we must behold: imprisonment by
the authorities; the third degree—and flagellation.

We conceive our man deciding that his career had
been perhaps too eventful.  Yet Penrod had condensed
all of it into eight hours.

It appears that he had at least some shadowy per-
ception of a recent fulness of life, for, as he leaned
against the fence, gazing upon his wistful Duke, he
sighed again and murmured aloud:

*"Well, hasn't this been a day!"*

But in a little while a star came out, freshly lighted,
from the highest part of the sky, and Penrod, looking
up, noticed it casualiy and a little drowsily.  He
yawned.  Then he sighed once more, but not reminis-
cently: evening had come; the day was over.

It was a sigh of pure *ennui*.

# SPRING IS HERE, WITH POEMS AND BATH TUBS

## By WILL ROGERS

Well, there has been quite a bit happened since I last communed with you. Spring is coming; I can tell by the Poetry and the Real Estate ads. A Poet exists all year just to get his Poem published in the Spring. Then when he sees it in print he starts getting next Spring's verse all ready. These early Spring Real Estate ads read, "This House is located on the shady banks of a Beautiful stream." Say, if there is a beautifull stream anywhere now the Rail Road runs along it and all you have to do is to get run over by a freight train to reach this beautiful stream.

A favorite ad is, "Beautiful Home in heart of the most exclusive Residential District, 5 Master Bedrooms and 9 baths; Owner going to Europe." Now let's just take that ad out and dissect it and see what it is.

In a Real Estate man's eye, the most exclusive part of the City is wherever he has a House to sell. The Dog Pound may be on one side and the City Incinerator on the other but it's still exclusive. And it is, too, for it will be the only house in the world so situated.

Five Master Bedrooms! Now, they get that Master junk from English ads where the man may be the

(Copyright, 1924, by Albert & Charles Boni, Inc., and McNaught Syndicate.)

master. Still, I don't know why they call all the
rooms his. Over here they call them Master Bedrooms
but the Wife will pick out the Poorest one for him,
and keep the other 4 Good ones for Company.

Now, to the ordinary man on reading that Ad of 9
Baths, that would be an insult to his cleanliness. A
Man would have to be awful Busy to support that
many Baths, unless, of course, he neglected some of
them. The ad might better have read, "Buy our
home and live in a Bath Tub." The biggest part of
City homes nowadays have more Baths than Beds. So,
while they can't always ask their Company to stay all
night as they have no place to put them, they can at
least ask them to Bathe. So, when you are invited
out now, you can always be assured of your private
Bath, but you must leave before Bed-time.

When you visit a friend's newly finished Home you
will be shown through all the Bath rooms, but when
you leave you couldn't, to save your soul, tell where
the dining room was. They seem to kinder want to
camouflage or hide that nowadays. There is such
little eating being done in the Homes now that a dining
room is almost a lost art. Breakfast is being served
in bed, Dinner at the Cabaret with dancing attached,
and lunch—no up-to-date Man would think of going
anywhere but to his Clubs for lunch. Besides, didn't
he hear a funny one and must get to the Club to bore
his alleged friends with it? He will talk everybody's
left ear off all day and come home and bite his Wife's
off if she asks him to tell her the news.

And then they have such an enlightening custom
nowadays. Every body of men who can think of a
name have a Club. And is not Congressman Blind-
bridle, who has just returned from a free Government

trip to Bermuda, going to deliver a Message at today's Luncheon on "Americanism, Or what we owe to the Flag"?

Now, as the dining room space has been eliminated to make room for an additional Bath, most of the eating, if one happens to be entertaining at home, is done off The Lap. This custom of slow starvation has shown vast improvement of late. Instead of the Napkins being of Paper, why, they have been supplanted by almost-linen ones with beautiful hemstitching. That's to try and get your mind off the lack of nourishment. As I say, the Napkin is hand sewn but the Lettuce Sandwiches still come from the Delicatessen.

Why, in the good old days, they couldn't have fed you on your lap 'cause you couldn't have held all they would give you. Now you have to feel for it to find it.

But the Husband does come home some time during the Day or Night, for is not the overhead on his outlay of Baths going on all the time, and shouldn't he be getting home to get some good out of some of them?

It's not the high cost of Living that is driving us to the Poor House,—It's the high Cost of bathing. The big question today is not what are you going to pay for your plot of ground, but what kind of fixtures are you going to put in your legion of Bath Rooms. Manufacturers of Porcelain and Tile have Supplanted the Pocket Flask as our principal commodity.

The interest on unpaid-for Bath Rooms would pay our National Debt.

Now, mind you, I am not against this modern accomplishment, or extravagance, of ours. I realize that

these Manufacturers of Fixtures have advanced their
Art to the point where they are practically modern
Michael Angelos. Where, in the old days, an Elephant
Hook was almost necessary for a Wife to drag her
Husband toward anything that looked like Water,
today those Interior Bath Decorators can almost make
one of those things inviting enough to get in without
flinching.

But, in doing so, they have destroyed an American
Institution, and ruined the only Calendar that a Child
ever had. That was the Saturday Night bath. Nowadays a Child just grows up in ignorance. From the
Cradle to the Altar he don't know what day of the week
it is. In those good old days he knew that the next
morning after that weekly Ear washing he was going
to Sunday School. Now he has not only eliminated
the Bath on Saturday but has practically eliminated
the Sunday School, for neither he nor his Parents
know when Sunday comes.

But, in those days, that old Kitchen Stove was kept
hot after supper. And not only the Tea kettle was
filled but other Pots and Pans, and the Family Wash
Tub was dragged up by the Fire, and you went out
to the Well and helped your Pa draw some Water
to mix with that hot. While you was doing that,
your Ma, if you stayed Lucky and had a Ma up to
then, was a getting out all the clean Clothes and a
fixing the Buttons, and a laying out the schedule of
who was to be first. And She was the only one could
tell just how much hot Water to put in to make it
right. And if anybody had to feel of the hot water
and get burned it was always her, not you, and she
found dirt behind, and in, your Ears that all the
highfaluting Fixtures in the World can't find today.

Now that was an event. It meant something. It brought you closer together. But now bathing is so common there's No Kick To It. It's just *Bla! !*

The Romans started this Bath Gag; now look what become of them. They used to have the most beautiful Baths, kind of a Municipal Bath, where they all met and strolled around and draped themselves on Marble Slabs. It was a kinder Society event. It compared to our modern Receptions. I have seen some beautiful Paintings of them, but I have yet to see a Scene where a Roman was in the Water. But they did look, oh, just too cunning, sunning themselves out on the Concrete Banks of those Pools. It must have been like visiting our modern Beaches, where no one can swim but the Life Guard, and they don't know that he can as he has never been called on to go in. But, like the Romans, our Girls can arrange themselves in the most bewitching shapes out on the sand, which, after all, must be much more comfortable than the Asphalt that those little Cæsars had to spread themselves over.

I tell you if Baths keep on multiplying in the modern Home as they have lately it won't be 5 Years till a Bath Tub will be as necessary in a home as a Cocktail Shaker.

If two members of the same household have to use the same Bath, it is referred to now as a Community Tub.

Statistics have proven that there are 25 Bath Tubs sold to every Bible.

And fifty to every Dictionary, and 380 to every Encyclopedia.

Proving that, while we may be neglecting the Interior, we are looking after the exterior.

If the Father of our Country, George Washington, was Tutankhamened tomorrow, and, after being aroused from his Tomb, was told that the American People today spend two Billion Dollars yearly on Bathing Material, he would say, "WHAT GOT 'EM SO DIRTY?"

# THE CUSTODY OF THE PUMPKIN

## By P. G. WODEHOUSE

The pleasant morning sunshine descended like an amber shower bath on Blandings Castle, that stately home of England which so adorns the county of Shropshire, lighting up with a heartening glow its ivied walls, its rolling parks, its gardens, outhouses and messuages and such of its inhabitants as chanced at the moment to be taking the air. It fell on green lawns and wide terraces, on noble trees and bright flower beds. It fell on the baggy trousers seat of Angus McAllister, head gardener to the Earl of Emsworth, as he bent with dour Scottish determination to pluck a coy snail from its reverie beneath the leaf of a lettuce. It fell on the white flannels of the Hon. Freddie Threepwood, Lord Emsworth's second son, hurrying across the water meadows. It also fell on Lord Emsworth himself, for the proprietor of this fair domain was standing on the turret above the west wing, placidly surveying his possessions through a powerful telescope.

The Earl of Emsworth was a fluffy-minded and amiable old gentleman with a fondness for new toys. Altho the main interest of his life was his garden, he was always ready to try a side line; and the latest of these side lines was this telescope of his—the out-

(Copyright, 1924, by Curtis Publishing Co.)

43

come of a passion for astronomy which had lasted some two weeks.

For some minutes Lord Emsworth remained gazing with a pleased eye at a cow down in the meadows. It was a fine cow, as cows go, but, like so many cows, it lacked sustained dramatic interest; and his lordship, surfeited after a while by the spectacle of it chewing the cud and staring glassily at nothing, was about to swivel the apparatus round in the hope of picking up something a trifle more sensational, when into the range of his vision there came the Honorable Freddie. White and shining, he tripped along over the turf like a Theocritean shepherd hastening to keep an appointment with a nymph; and for the first time that morning a frown came to mar the serenity of Lord Emsworth's brow. He generally frowned when he saw Freddie, for with the passage of the years that youth had become more and more of a problem to an anxious father.

The Earl of Emsworth, like so many of Britain's aristocracy, had but little use for the Younger Son. And Freddie Threepwood was a particularly trying younger son. There seemed, in the opinion of his nearest and dearest, to be no way of coping with the boy. If he was allowed to live in London he piled up debts and got into mischief; and when hauled back home to Blandings he moped broodingly. It was possibly the fact that his demeanor at this moment was so mysteriously jaunty, his bearing so inexplicably free from the crushed misery with which he usually mooned about the place that induced Lord Emsworth to keep a telescopic eye on him. Some inner voice whispered to him that Freddie was up to no good and would bear watching.

The inner voice was absolutely correct. Within thirty seconds its case had been proved up to the hilt. Scarcely had his lordship had time to wish, as he invariably wished on seeing his offspring, that Freddie had been something entirely different in manners, morals and appearance and had been the son of somebody else living a considerable distance away, when out of a small spinney near the end of the meadow there bounded a girl. And Freddie, after a cautious glance over his shoulder, immediately proceeded to fold this female in a warm embrace.

Lord Emsworth had seen enough. He tottered away from the telescope, a shattered man. One of his favorite dreams was of some nice eligible girl, belonging to a good family and possessing a bit of money of her own, coming along some day and taking Freddie off his hands; but that inner voice, more confident now than ever, told him that this was not she. Freddie would not sneak off in this furtive fashion to meet eligible girls; nor could he imagine any eligible girl in her right senses rushing into Freddie's arms in that enthusiastic way. No, there was only one explanation. In the cloistral seclusion of Blandings, far from the metropolis with all its conveniences for that sort of thing, Freddie had managed to get himself entangled. Seething with anguish and fury, Lord Emsworth hurried down the stairs and out onto the terrace. Here he prowled like an elderly leopard waiting for feeding time, until in due season there was a flicker of white among the trees that flanked the drive and a cheerful whistling announced the culprit's approach.

It was with a sour and hostile eye that Lord Emsworth watched his son draw near. He adjusted his pince-nez, and with their assistance was able to perceive that a fatuous smile of self-satisfaction illuminated the young man's face, giving him the appearance of a beaming sheep. In the young man's buttonhole there shone a nosegay of simple meadow flowers, which, as he walked, he patted from time to time with a loving hand.

"Frederick!" bellowed his lordship.

The villain of the piece halted abruptly. Sunk in a roseate trance, he had not observed his father. But such was the sunniness of his mood that even this encounter could not damp him. He gamboled happily up.

"Hullo, guv'nor," said Freddie. He searched in his mind for a pleasant topic of conversation, always a matter of some little difficulty on these occasions. "Lovely day, what?"

His lordship was not to be diverted into a discussion of the weather. He drew a step nearer, looking like the man who smothered the young princes in the Tower.

"Frederick," he demanded, "who was that girl?"

The Honorable Freddie started convulsively. He appeared to be swallowing with difficulty something large and jagged.

"Girl?" he quavered. "Girl? Girl, guv'nor?"

"That girl I saw you kissing ten minutes ago down in the water meadows."

"Oh!" said the Honorable Freddie. He paused. "Oh, ah!" He paused again. "Oh, ah, yes! I've been meaning to tell you about that, guv'nor."

"You have, have you?"

"All perfectly correct, you know. Oh, yes, indeed!

All most absolutely correct-o! Nothing fishy, I mean to say, or anything like that. She's my fiancée."

A sharp howl escaped Lord Emsworth, as if one of the bees humming in the lavender beds had taken time off to sting him in the neck.

"Who is she?" he boomed. "Who is this woman?"

"Her name's Donaldson."

"Who is she?"

"Aggie Donaldson. Aggie's short for Niagara. Her people spent their honeymoon at the Falls, she tells me. She's American, and all that. Rummy names they give kids in America," proceeded Freddie with hollow chattiness. "I mean to say! Niagara! I ask you!"

"Who is she?"

"She's most awfully bright, you know. Full of beans. You'll love her."

"Who is she?"

"And can play the saxophone."

"Who," demanded Lord Emsworth for the sixth time, "is she? And where did you meet her?"

Freddie coughed. The information, he perceived, could no longer be withheld, and he was keenly alive to the fact that it scarcely fell into the class of tidings of great joy.

"Well, as a matter of fact, guv-nor, she's a sort of cousin of Angus McAllister's. She's come over to England for a visit, don't you know, and is staying with the old boy. That's how I happened to run across her."

Lord Emsworth's eyes bulged and he gargled faintly. He had had many unpleasant visions of his son's future, but they had never included one of him walk-

ing down the aisle with a sort of cousin of his head
gardener.

"Oh!" he said. "Oh, indeed?"

Lord Emsworth threw his arms up as if calling on
heaven to witness a good man's persecution, and shot
off along the terrace at a rapid trot. Having ranged
the grounds for some minutes, he ran his quarry to
earth at the entrance of the yew alley.

The head gardener turned at the sound of his
footsteps. He was a sturdy man of medium height
with eyebrows that would have fitted better a bigger
forehead. These, added to a red and wiry beard,
gave him a formidable and uncompromising expression. Honesty Angus McAllister's face had in full
measure, and also intelligence; but it was a bit short
on sweetness and light.

"McAllister," said his lordship, plunging without
preamble into the matter of his discourse. "That
girl. You must send her away." A look of bewilderment clouded such of Mr. McAllister's features as
were not concealed behind his beard and eyebrows.

"Gurrul?"

"That girl who is staying with you. She must go!"

"Gae where?"

Lord Emsworth was not in the mood to be finicky
about details.

"Anywhere," he said. "I won't have her here a
day longer."

"Why?" inquired Mr. McAllister, who liked to
thresh these things out.

"Never mind why. You must send her away immediately."

Mr. McAllister mentioned an insuperable objection.

"She's payin' me twa poon' a week," he said simply.

Lord Emsworth did not grind his teeth, for he was not given to that form of displaying emotion; but he leaped some ten inches into the air and dropped his pince-nez. And, tho normally a fair-minded and reasonable man, well aware that modern earls must think twice before pulling the feudal stuff on their employees, he took on the forthright truculence of a large landowner of the early Norman period ticking off a serf.

"Listen, McAllister! Listen to me! Either you send that girl away to-day or you can go yourself."

A curious expression came into Angus McAllister's face—always excepting the occupied territories. It was the look of a man who has not forgotten Bannockburn, a man conscious of belonging to the country of William Wallace and Robert the Bruce. He made Scotch noises at the back of his throat.

"Y'r lorrudsheep will accept ma notis," he said with formal dignity.

"I'll pay you a month's wages in lieu of notice and you will leave this afternoon," retorted Lord Emsworth with spirit.

"Mphm!" said Mr. McAllister.

Lord Emsworth left the battlefield with a feeling of pure exhilaration, still in the grip of the animal fury of conflict. No twinge of remorse did he feel at the thought that Angus McAllister had served him faithfully for ten years. Nor did it cross his mind that he might miss McAllister.

But that night, as he sat smoking his after-dinner cigaret, Reason, so violently expelled, came stealing timidly back to her throne, and a cold hand seemed suddenly placed upon his heart.

With Angus McAllister gone, how would the pumpkin fare?

The importance of this pumpkin in the Earl of
Emsworth's life requires, perhaps, a word of explanation. Every ancient family in England has some
little gap in its scroll of honor, and that of Lord
Emsworth was no exception. For generations back
his ancestors had been doing notable deeds; they had
sent out from Blandings Castle statesmen and war-
riors, governors and leaders of the people; but they
had not—in the opinion of the present holder of
the title—achieved a full hand. However splendid
the family record might appear at first sight, the fact
remained that no Earl of Emsworth had ever won a
first prize for pumpkins at the Shrewsbury Flower
and Vegetable Show. For roses, yes. For tulips,
true. For spring onions, granted. But not for pumpkins; and Lord Emsworth, who lived for his garden,
felt it deeply.

For many a summer past he had been striving in-
defatigably to remove this blot on the family escutch-
eon, only to see his hopes go tumbling down. But
this year at last victory had seemed in sight, for there
had been vouchsafed to Blandings a competitor of
such amazing parts that his lordship, who had watched
it grow practically from a pip, could not envisage
failure. Surely, he told himself as he gazed on its
golden roundness, even Sir Gregory Parsloe-Parsloe
of Badgwick Hall, winner for three successive years,
would never be able to produce anything to challenge
this superb vegetable.

And it was this supreme pumpkin whose welfare
he feared he had jeopardized by dismissing Angus
McAllister. For Angus was its official trainer. He

understood the pumpkin. Indeed, in his reserved Scottish way he even seemed to love it. With Angus gone, what would the harvest be?

Such were the meditations of Lord Emsworth as he reviewed the position of affairs. And tho, as the days went by, he tried to tell himself that Angus McAllister was not the only man in the world who understood pumpkins and that he had every confidence, the most complete and unswerving confidence, in Robert Barker, recently Angus' second in command, now promoted to the post of head gardener and custodian of the Blandings Hope, he knew that this was but shallow bravado. When you are a pumpkin owner with a big winner in your stable, you judge men by hard standards, and every day it became plainer that Robert Barker was only a makeshift. Within a week Lord Emsworth was pining for Angus McAllister.

It might be purely imagination, but to his excited fancy the pumpkin seemed to be pining for Angus too. It appeared to be dropping and losing weight. Lord Emsworth could not rid himself of the horrible idea that it was shrinking. And on the tenth night after McAllister's departure he dreamed a strange dream. He had gone with King George to show his gracious majesty the pumpkin, promising him the treat of a lifetime; and, when they arrived, there in the corner of the frame was a shriveled thing the size of a pea. He woke, sweating, with his sovereign's disappointed screams ringing in his ears; and Pridge gave its last quiver and collapsed. To reinstate Angus would be a surrender, but it must be done.

"Beach," he said that morning at breakfast, "do you happen to—er—to have McAllister's address?"

"Yes, your lordship," replied the butler. "He is in London, residing at Number 11 Buxton Crescent."

"Buxton Crescent? Never heard of it."

"It is, I fancy, your lordship, a boarding house or some such establishment off the Cromwell Road. McAllister was accustomed to make it his headquarters whenever he visited the metropolis on account of its handiness for Kensington Gardens. He liked," said Beach with respectful reproach, for Angus had been a friend of his for nine years, "to be near the flowers, your lor'ship."

Two telegrams, passing through it in the course of the next twelve hours, caused some gossip at the post office of the little town of Market Blandings.

The first ran: "McAllister, 11 Buxton Crescent, Cromwell Road, London. Return immediately. Emsworth."

The second: "Lord Emsworth, Blandings Castle, Shropshire. I will not. McAllister."

Lord Emsworth had one of those minds capable of accommodating but one thought at a time—if that; and the possibility that Angus McAllister might decline to return had not occurred to him. It was difficult to adjust himself to this new problem, but he managed it at last. Before nightfall he had made up his mind. Robert Barker, that broken reed, could remain in charge for another day or so, and meanwhile he would go up to London and engage a real head gardener, the finest head gardener that money could buy.

It was the opinion of Doctor Johnson that there is in London all that life can afford. A man, he held, who is tired of London is tired of life itself. Lord Emsworth, had he been aware of this statement, would have contested it warmly. He hated London. He loathed its crowds, its smells, its noises; its omnibuses, its taxis and its hard pavements. And, in addition to all its other defects, the miserable town did not seem able to produce a single decent head gardener. He went from agency to agency, interviewing candidates, and not one of them came within a mile of meeting his requirements. He disliked their faces, he distrusted their references. It was a harsh thing to say of any man, but he was dashed if the best of them was even as good as Robert Barker.

It was, therefore, in a black and soured mood that his lordship, having lunched frugally at the Senior Conservative Club on the third day of his visit, stood on the steps in the sunshine, wondering how on earth he was to get through the afternoon. He had spent the morning rejecting head gardeners, and the next batch was not due until the morrow. And what—besides rejecting head gardeners—was there for a man of reasonable tastes to do with his time in this hopeless town?

And then there came into his mind a remark which Beach the butler had made at the breakfast table about flowers in Kensington Gardens. He could go to Kensington Gardens and look at the flowers.

He was about to hail a taxicab from the rank down the street when there suddenly emerged from the Hotel Magnificent, over the way, a young man. This man proceeded to cross the road, and as he drew near it seemed to Lord Emsworth that there was about his appearance something oddly familiar. He stared for a long instant before he could believe his eyes, then with a wordless cry bounded down the steps just as the other started to mount them.

"Oh. hullo, guv'nor!" ejaculated the Honorable Freddie, plainly startled.

"What—what are you doing here?" demanded Lord Emsworth.

He spoke with heat, and justly so. London, as the result of several spirited escapades which still rankled in the mind of a father who had had to foot the bills, was forbidden ground to Freddie.

The young man was plainly not at his ease. He had the air of one who is being pushed toward dangerous machinery in which he is loath to become entangled. He shuffled his feet for a moment, then raised his left shoe and rubbed the back of his right calf with it. "The fact is, guv'nor——"

"You know you are forbidden to come to London."

"Absolutely, guv'nor, but the fact is——"

"And why anybody but an imbecile should want to come to London when he could be at Blandings——"

"I know, guv'nor, but the fact is——" Here Freddie, having replaced his wandering foot on the pavement, raised the other and rubbed the back of his left calf. "I wanted to see you," he said. "Yes. Particularly wanted to see you."

This was not strictly accurate. The last thing in the world which the Honorable Freddie wanted was to see his parent. He had come to the Senior Conservative Club to leave a carefully written note. Having delivered which, it had been his intention to bolt like a rabbit. This unforeseen meeting had upset his plans.

"To see me?" said Lord Emsworth. "Why?"

"Got—er—got something to tell you. Bit of news."

"I trust it is of sufficient importance to justify your coming to London against my express wishes."

"Oh, yes. Oh, yes, yes, yes. Oh, rather. It's dashed important. Yes—not to put too fine a point upon it—most dashed important. I say, guv'nor, are you in fairly good form to stand a bit of a shock?"

A ghastly thought rushed into Lord Emsworth's mind. Freddie's mysterious arrival—his strange manner—his odd hesitation and uneasiness— Could it mean? He clutched the young man's arm feverishly.

"Frederick! Speak! Tell me! Have the cats got at it?"

It was a fixed idea of Lord Emsworth, which no argument would have induced him to abandon, that cats had the power to work some dreadful mischief on his pumpkin and were continually lying in wait for the opportunity of doing so; and his behavior on the occasion when one of the fast sporting set from the stables, wandering into the kitchen garden and, finding him gazing at the Blandings Hope, had rubbed itself sociably against his leg, lingered long in that animal's memory.

Freddie stared.

"Cats? Why? Where? Which? What cats?"

"Frederick! Is anything wrong with the pumpkin?"

In a crass and materialistic world there must inevitably be a scattered few here and there in whom pumpkins touch no chord. The Hon. Freddie Threepwood was one of these. He was accustomed to speak in mockery of all pumpkins, and had even gone so far as to allude to the Hope of Blandings as Percy.

His father's anxiety, therefore, merely caused him to giggle.

"Not that I know of," he said.

"Then what do you mean," thundered Lord Emsworth, stung by the giggle—"what do you mean, sir, by coming here and alarming me—scaring me out of my wits, by gad!—with your nonsense about giving me shocks?"

The Honorable Freddie looked carefully at his fermenting parent. His fingers, sliding into his pocket, closed on the note which nestled there. He drew it forth.

"Look here, guv'nor," he said nervously, "I think the best thing would be for you to read this. Meant to leave it for you with the hall porter. It's—well, you just cast your eyes over it. Good-by, guv'nor. Got to see a man."

And thrusting the note into his father's hand the Honorable Freddie turned and was gone. Lord Emsworth, perplexed and annoyed, watched him skim up the road and leap into a cab. He seethed impotently. Practically any behavior on the part of his son Frederick had the power to irritate him, but it was when he was vague and mysterious and incoherent that the young man irritated him most.

He looked at the letter in his hand, turned it over, felt it and even smelt it. Then, for it had suddenly occurred to him that if he wished to ascertain its contents he had better read it, he tore open the envelope.

The note was brief, but full of good reading matter.

*"Dear Guv'nor:* Awfully sorry, and all that, but couldn't hold out any longer. I've popped up to

London in the two-seater, and Aggie and I were spliced this morning. There looked like being a bit of a hitch at one time, but Aggie's guv'nor, who has come over from America, managed to wangle it all right by getting a special license or something of that order. A most capable Johnny. He's coming to see you. He wants to have a good long talk with you about the whole binge. Lush him up hospitably, and all that, would you mind, because he's a really sound egg and you'll like him.

"Well, cheerio!

"Your affectionate son,

"Freddie.

"P. S. You won't mind if I freeze onto the two-seater for the nonce, what? It may come in useful for the honeymoon."

The Senior Conservative Club is a solid and massive building, but, as Lord Emsworth raised his eyes dumbly from the perusal of this letter, it seemed to him that it was performing a kind of whirling dance. The whole of the immediate neighborhood, indeed, appeared to be shimmying in the middle of a thick mist. He was profoundly stirred. It is not too much to say that he was shaken to the core of his being. No father enjoys being flouted and defied by his own son; nor is it reasonable to expect a man to take a cheery view of life who is faced with the prospect of supporting for the remainder of his years a younger son, a younger son's wife and possibly younger grandchildren.

For an appreciable space of time he stood in the middle of the pavement, rooted to the spot. Passers-by bumped into him or grumblingly made detours

to avoid a collision. Dogs sniffed at his ankles.
Seedy-looking individuals tried to arrest his attention
in order to speak of their financial affairs. Lord Emsworth heeded none of them. He remained where
he was, gaping like a fish, until suddenly his faculties
seemed to return to him.

An imperative need for flowers and green trees
swept upon Lord Emsworth. The noise of the traffic
and the heat of the sun on the stone pavement were
afflicting him like a nightmare. He signaled ener-
getically to a passing cab.

"Kensington Gardens," he said, and sank back on
the cushioned seat.

Something dimly resembling peace crept into his
lordship's soul as he paid off his cab and entered the
cool shade of the gardens. Even from the road he
had caught a glimpse of stimulating reds and yellows;
and as he ambled up the asphalt path and plunged
round the corner the flower beds burst upon his sight
in all their consoling glory.

"Ah!" breathed Lord Emsworth rapturously, and
came to a halt before a glowing carpet of tulips. A
man of official aspect, wearing a peaked cap and a
uniform, stopped as he heard the exclamation and
looked at him with approval and even affection.

"Nice weather we're 'avin," he observed.

Lord Emsworth did not reply. He had not heard.
There is that about a well-set-out bed of flowers
which acts on men who love their gardens like a
drug, and he was in a sort of trance. Already he
had completely forgotten where he was, and seemed
to himself to be back in his paradise of Blandings.
He drew a step nearer to the flower bed, pointing
like a setter.

The official-looking man's approval deepened. This man with the peaked cap was the park keeper, who held the rights of the high, the low and the middle justice over that section of the gardens. He, too, loved these flower beds, and he seemed to see in Lord Emsworth a kindred soul. The general public was too apt to pass by, engrossed in its own affairs, and this often wounded the park keeper. In Lord Emsworth he thought that he recognized one of the right sort.

"Nice——" he began.

He broke off with a sharp cry. If he had not seen it with his own eyes he would not have believed it. But, alas, there was no possibility of a mistake. With a ghastly shock he realized that he had been deceived in this attractive stranger. Decently if untidily dressed, clean, respectable to the outward eye, the stranger was in reality a dangerous criminal, the blackest type of evildoer on the park keeper's index. He was a Kensington Gardens flower picker.

For, even as he uttered the word "nice," the man had stepped lightly over the low railing, had shambled across the strip of turf, and before you could say "knife" was busy on his dark work. In the brief instant in which the park keeper's vocal cords refused to obey him, he was two tulips ahead of the game and reaching out to scoop in a third.

"Hi!" roared the park keeper, suddenly finding speech. "'I there!"

Lord Emsworth turned with a start.

"Bless my soul!" he murmured reproachfully.

He was in full possession of his senses now, such as they were, and understood the enormity of his conduct. He shuffled back onto the asphalt, contrite.

"My dear fellow——" he began remorsefully.

The park keeper began to speak rapidly and at length. From time to time Lord Emsworth moved his lips and made deprecating gestures, but he could not stem the flood. Louder and more rhetorical grew the park keeper, and denser and more interested the rapidly assembling crowd of spectators. And then through the stream of words another voice spoke.

"Wot's all this?"

The force had materialized in the shape of a large, solid constable.

The park keeper seemed to understand that he had been superseded. He still spoke, but no longer like a father rebuking an erring son. His attitude now was more that of an elder brother appealing for justice against a delinquent junior. In a moving passage he stated his case.

"'E says," observed the constable judicially, speaking slowly and in capitals as if addressing an untutored foreigner—"'E says you was pickin' the flowers."

"I saw 'im. I was standin' as close as I am to you."

"'E saw you," interpreted the constable.

Lord Emsworth was feeling weak and bewildered. Without a thought of annoying or doing harm to anybody, he seemed to have unchained the fearful passions of a French Revolution; and there came over him a sense of how unjust it was that this sort of thing should be happening to him, of all people— a man already staggering beneath the troubles of a Job.

"I'll 'ave to ask you for your name and address," said the constable more briskly. A stubby pencil

popped for an instant into his stern mouth and
hovered, well and truly moistened, over the virgin
page of his notebook—that dreadful notebook before
which taxi drivers shrink and hardened bus con-
ductors quail.

"I—I, why, my dear fellow—I mean, officer—I
am the Earl of Emsworth."

Much has been written of the psychology of crowds,
designed to show how extraordinary and inexplicable
it is, but most of such writing is exaggeration. A
crowd generally behaves in a perfectly natural and
intelligible fashion. When, for instance, it sees a
man in a badly fitting tweed suit and a hat he ought
to be ashamed of getting put through it for pinching
flowers in the park and the man says he is an earl,
it laughs. This crowd laughed.

"Ho?" The constable did not stoop to join in
the merriment of the rabble, but his lip twitched
sardonically. "Have you a card, your lordship?"

Nobody intimate with Lord Emsworth would have
asked such a foolish question. His cardcase was the
thing he always lost second when visiting London—
immediately after losing his umbrella.

"I—er—I'm afraid——"

"R!" said the constable. And the crowd uttered
another happy, hyenalike laugh, so intensely galling
that his lordship raised his bowed head and found
enough spirit to cast an indignant glance. And as he
did so the hunted look faded from his eyes.

"McAllister!" he cried. "McAllister, my dear fellow, do please tell this man who I am."

Two new arrivals had just joined the throng, and,
being of rugged and nobbly physique, had already
shoved themselves through to the ringside seats. One

was a tall, handsome, smooth-faced gentleman of authoritative appearance, who, if he had not worn rimless glasses, would have looked like a Roman emperor. The other was a shorter, sturdier man with a bristly red beard.

"McAllister!" moaned his lordship piteously.

After what had passed between himself and his late employer a lesser man than Angus McAllister might have seen in Lord Emsworth's predicament merely a judgment. A man of little magnanimity would have felt that here was where he got a bit of his own back. Not so this splendid Glaswegian.

"Aye," he said. "Yon's Lorrud Emsworuth."

"Who are you?" inquired the constable searchingly.

"I used to be head gardener at the cassel."

"Exactly," bleated Lord Emsworth. "Precisely. My head gardener."

The constable was shaken. Lord Emsworth might not look like an earl, but there was no getting away from the fact that Angus McAllister was supremely head-gardeneresque. A staunch admirer of the aristocracy, the constable perceived that zeal had caused him to make a bit of a bloomer. Yes, he had dropped a brick.

In this crisis, however. he comported himself with a masterly tact. He scowled blackly upon the interested throng.

"Pass along there, please. Pass along." he commanded austerely. "Ought to know better than block up a public thoroughfare like this. Pass along!"

He moved off, shepherding the crowd before him. The Roman emperor with the rimless glasses advanced upon Lord Emsworth, extending a large hand.

"Pleased to meet you at last," he said. "My name is Donaldson, Lord Emsworth."

For a moment the name conveyed nothing to his lordship. Then its significance hit him, and he drew himself up with hauteur.

"You'll excuse us, Angus," said Mr. Donaldson. "High time you and I had a little chat, Lord Emsworth."

Lord Emsworth was about to speak, when he caught the other's eye. It was a strong, keen, level gray eye, with a curious forcefulness about it that made him feel strangely inferior. There is every reason to suppose that Mr. Donaldson had subscribed for years to those personality courses advertised in the back pages of the magazines, which guarantee to impart to the pupil who takes ten correspondence lessons the ability to look the boss in the eye and make him wilt. Mr. Donaldson looked Lord Emsworth in the eye, and Lord Emsworth wilted.

"How do you do?" he said weakly.

"Now listen, Lord Emsworth," proceeded Mr. Donaldson. "No sense in having hard feelings between members of a family. I take it you've heard by this that your boy and my girl have gone ahead and fixed it up? Personally, I'm delighted. That boy is a fine young fellow——"

Lord Emsworth blinked.

"You are speaking of my son Frederick?" he said incredulously.

"Of your son Frederick. Now, at the moment, no doubt, you are feeling a trifle sore. I don't blame you. You have every right to be sorer than a gumboil. But you must remember—young blood, eh?

It will, I am convinced, be a lasting grief to that splendid young man——"

"You are still speaking of my son Frederick?"

"Of Frederick, yes. It will, I say, be a lasting grief to him if he feels he has incurred your resentment. You must forgive him, Lord Emsworth. He must have your support."

"I suppose he'll have to have it, dash it," said his lordship unhappily. "Can't let the boy starve."

Mr. Donaldson's hand swept round in a wide grand gesture.

"Don't you worry about that. I'll look after that end of it. I am not a rich man——"

"Ah!" said his lordship resignedly. A faint hope, inspired by the largeness of the other's manner, had been flickering in his bosom.

"I doubt," continued Mr. Donaldson frankly, "if, all told, I have as much as ten million dollars in the world."

Lord Emsworth swayed like a sapling in the breeze.

"Ten million? Ten million? Did you say you had ten million dollars?"

"Between nine and ten, I suppose. Not more. But you must bear in mind that the business is growing all the time. I am Donaldson's Dog Biscuits."

"Donaldson's Dog Biscuits! Indeed! Really! Fancy that!"

"You have heard of them?" asked Mr. Donaldson eagerly.

"Never," said Lord Emsworth cordially.

"Oh! Well, that's who I am. And, with your approval, I intend to send Frederick over to Long Island City to start learning the business. I have

chronicle there may be one or two who for various reasons found themselves unable to attend the annual Flower and Vegetable Show at Shrewsbury. Sir Gregory Parsloe-Parsloe of Badgwick Hall was there, of course, but it would not have escaped the notice of a close observer that his mien lacked something of the haughty arrogance which had characterized it in other years. From time to time, as he paced the tent devoted to the exhibition of vegetables, he might have been seen to bite his lip, and his eye had something of that brooding look which Napoleon's must have worn after Waterloo.

But there is the right stuff in Sir Gregory. He is a gentleman and a sportsman. In the Parsloe-Parsloe tradition there is nothing small or mean. Halfway down the tent he stopped, and with a quick manly gesture thrust out his hand.

"Congratulate you, Emsworth," he said huskily.

Lord Emsworth looked up with a start. He had been deep in his thoughts.

"Thanks, my dear fellow. Thanks. Thanks. Thank you very much." He hesitated. "Er—can't both win, if you understand me."

Sir Gregory puzzled it out.

"No," he said. "No. See what you mean. Can't both win."

He nodded and walked on, with who knows what vultures gnawing at his broad bosom? And Lord Emsworth—with Angus McAllister, who had been a silent witness of the scene, at his side—turned once more to stare reverently at that which lay on the strawy bottom of one of the largest packing cases ever seen in Shrewsbury town.

Inside it, something vast and golden beamed up at him.

A card had been attached to the exterior of the packing case. It bore the simple legend:

PUMPKINS.  FIRST PRIZE.

# THE ACCURSED HOUSE

## By Emile Gaboriau

The Vicomte de B———, an amiable and charming young man, was peacefully enjoying an income of 30,000 livres yearly, when, unfortunately for him, his uncle, a miser of the worst species, died, leaving him all his wealth, amounting to nearly two millions.

In running through the documents of succession, the Vicomte de B——— learned that he was the proprietor of a house in the Rue de la Victoire. He learned, also, that the unfurnished building, bought in 1849 for 300,000 francs, now brought in, clear of taxes, rentals amounting to 82,000 francs a year.

"Too much, too much, entirely," thought the generous vicomte, "my uncle was too hard; to rent at this price is usury, one can not deny it. When one bears a great name like mine, one should not lend himself to such plundering. I will begin tomorrow to lower my rents, and my tenants will bless me."

With this excellent purpose in view, the Vicomte de B——— sent immediately for the *concièrge* of the building, who presented himself as promptly, with back bent like a bow.

"Bernard, my friend," said the vicomte, "go at once from me and notify all your tenants that I lower their rents by one-third."

That unheard-of word "lower" fell like a brick on

(Copyright, 1891, by The Current Literature Publishing Co. Translated by E. C. Waggener.)

Bernard's head. But he quickly recovered himself; he had heard badly; he had not understood.

"Low—er the rents!" stammered he. "Monsieur le Vicomte deigns to jest. Lower! Monsieur, of course means to raise the rents."

"I was never more serious in my life, my friend," the vicomte returned; "I said, and I repeat it, lower the rents."

This time the *concièrge* was surprised to the point of bewilderment—so thrown off his balance that he forgot himself and lost all restraint.

"Monsieur has not reflected," persisted he. "Monsieur will regret this evening. Lower the tenants' rents! Never was such a thing known, monsieur! If the lodgers should learn of it, what would they think of monsieur? What would people say in the neighborhood? Truly—"

"Monsieur Bernard, my friend," dryly interrupted the vicomte, "I prefer, when I give an order, to be obeyed without reply. You hear me—go!"

Staggering like a drunken man, Monsieur Bernard went out from the house of his proprietor.

All his ideas were upset, overthrown, confounded. Was he, or was he not, the plaything of a dream, a ridiculous nightmare? Was he himself Pierre Bernard, or Bernard somebody else?

"Lower his rents! lower his rents!" repeated he. "It is not to be believed! If indeed the lodgers had complained! But they have not complained; on the contrary, all are good prayers. Ah, if his uncle could only know this, he would rise from the tomb! His nephew has gone mad, 'tis certain! Lower the rents! They should have up this young man before a family council; he will finish badly! Who knows—

after this—what he will do next? He lunched too well, perhaps, this morning."

And the worthy Bernard was so pale with emotion when he reentered his lodge, so pale and spent, that on seeing him enter, his wife and daughter Amanda exclaimed as with one voice:

"Goodness! what is it? What has happened to you now?"

"Nothing," responded he, with altered voice, "absolutely nothing."

"You are deceiving me," insisted Madame Bernard, "you are concealing something from me; do not spare me; speak, I am strong—what did the new proprietor tell you? Does he think of turning us off?"

"If it were only that! But just think, he told me with his own lips, he told me to—ah! you will never believe me—"

"Oh, yes; only do go on."

"You will have it, then!— Well, then, he told me, he ordered me to notify all the tenants that—*he lowered their rents one-third!* Did you hear what I said?—*lowered* the rents of the tenants—"

But neither Madame nor Mademoiselle Bernard heard him out—they were twisting and doubling with convulsive laughter.

"Lower!" repeated they; "ah! what a good joke, what a droll man! Lower the tenants' rents."

But Bernard, losing his temper and insisting that he must be taken seriously in his own lodge, his wife lost her temper too, and a quarrel followed! Madame Bernard declaring that Monsieur Bernard had, beyond a doubt, taken his fantastic order from the bottom of a liter of wine in the restaurant at the corner.

But for Mademoiselle Amanda the couple would undoubtedly have come to blows, and finally Madame Bernard, who did not wish to be thought demented, threw a shawl over her head and ran to the proprietor's house. Bernard had spoken truly; with her own two ears, ornamented with big, gilded hoops, she heard the incredible word. Only, as she was a wise and prudent woman, she demanded "a bit of writing" to put, as she said, "her responsibility under cover."

She, too, returned thunderstruck, and all the evening in the lodge, father, mother, and daughter deliberated.

Should they obey? or should they warn some relative of this mad young man, whose common sense would oppose itself to such insanity?

They decided to obey.

Next morning, Bernard, buttoning himself into his best frock coat, made the rounds of the three-and-twenty lodges to announce his great news.

Ten minutes afterward the house in the Rue de la Victoire was in a state of commotion impossible to describe. People who, for forty years, had lived on the same floor, and never honored each other with so much as a tip of the hat, now clustered together and chatted eagerly.

"Do you know, monsieur?"

"It is very extraordinary."

"Simply unheard of!"

"The proprietor's lowered my rent!"

"One-third, is it not? Mine also."

"Astounding! It *must* be a mistake!"

And despite the affirmations of the Bernard family, despite even the "bit of writing" "under cover," there were found among the tenants doubting Thomases, who doubted still in the face of everything.

Three of them actually wrote to the proprietor to tell him what had passed, and to charitably warn him that his *concierge* had wholly lost his mind. The proprietor responded to these skeptics, confirming what Bernard had said. Doubt, therefore, was out of the question.

Then began reflections and commentaries.

"*Why* had the proprietor lowered his rents?"

"Yes, *why?*"

"What motives," said they all, "actuate this strange man? For certainly he must have grave reasons for a step like this! An intelligent man, a man of good sense, would never deprive himself of good fat revenues, well secured, for the simple pleasure of depriving himself. One would not conduct himself thus without being forced, constrained by powerful or terrible circumstances."

And each said to himself:

"*There is something under all this!*"

"But what?"

And from the first floor to the sixth they sought and conjectured and delved in their brains. Every lodger had the preoccupied air of a man that strives with all his wits to solve an impossible cipher, and everywhere there began to be a vague disquiet, as it happens when one finds himself in the presence of a sinister mystery.

Some one went so far as to hazard:

"This man must have committed a great and still hidden crime; remorse pushes him to philanthropy."

"It was not a pleasant idea, either, the thought of living thus side by side with a rascal; no, by no means; he might be repentant, and all that, but suppose he yielded to temptation once more!"

"The house, perhaps, was badly built?" questioned another, anxiously.

"Hum-m, so-so! no one could tell; but all knew one thing—it was very, very old!"

"True! and it had been necessary to prop it when they dug the drain last year in the month of March."

"Maybe it was the roof, then, and the house is top-heavy?" suggested a tenant on the fifth floor.

"Or perhaps," said a lodger in the garret, "there is a press for coining counterfeit money in the cellar; I have often heard at night a sound like the dull, muffled thud of a coin-stamper."

The opinion of another was that Russian, maybe Prussian, spies had gained a lodgment in the house, while the gentleman of the first story was inclined to believe that the proprietor purposed to set fire to his house and furniture with the sole object of drawing great sums from the insurance companies.

Then began to happen, as they all declared, extraordinary and even frightful things. On the sixth and mansard floors it appeared that strange and absolutely inexplicable noises were heard. Then the nurse of the old lady on the fourth story, going one night to steal wine from the cellar, encountered the ghost of the defunct proprietor—he even held in his hand a receipt for rent—by which she knew him!

And the refrain from aloft to cellar was:

"There *is* something under all this!"

From disquietude it had come to fright; from fright it quickly passed to terror. So that the gentleman of the first floor, who had valuables in his rooms, made up his mind to go, and sent in notice by his clerk.

Bernard went to inform the proprietor, who responded:

"All right, let the fool go!"

But next day the chiropodist of the second floor, tho he had naught to fear for his valuables, imitated the gentleman beneath him. Then the bachelors and the little households of the fifth story quickly followed his example.

From that moment it was a general rout. By the end of the week, everybody had given notice. Every one awaited some frightful catastrophe. They slept no more. They organized patrols. The terrified domestics swore that they too would quit the accursed house and remained temporarily only on tripled wages.

Bernard was no more than the ghost of himself; the fever of fear had worn him to a shadow.

"No," repeated his wife mournfully at each fresh notification, "no, it is *not* natural."

Meanwhile three-and-twenty "For Rent" placards swung against the facade of the house, drawing an occasional applicant for lodgings.

Bernard—never grumbling now—climbed the staircase and ushered the visitor from apartment to apartment.

"You can have your choice," said he to the people that presented themselves, "the house is entirely vacant; all the tenants have given notice as one man. They do not know why, exactly, but things have happened, oh! yes, *things!* a mystery such as was never before known—*the proprietor has lowered his rents!*"

And the would-be lodgers fled away affrighted.

The term ended, three-and-twenty vans carried away the furniture of the three-and-twenty tenants. Everybody left. From top to bottom, from foundations to garret, the house lay empty of lodgers.

The rats themselves, finding nothing to live on, abandoned it also.

Only the *concièrge* remained, gray green with fear in his lodge. Frightful visions haunted his sleep. He seemed to hear lugubrious howlings and sinister murmurs at night that made his teeth chatter with terror and his hair erect itself under his cotton nightcap. Madame Bernard no more closed an eye than he. And Amanda in her frenzy renounced all thought of the operatic stage and married—for nothing in the world but to quit the paternal lodge—a young barber and hair-dresser whom she had never before been able to abide.

At last, one morning, after a more frightful nightmare than usual, Bernard, too, took a great resolution. He went to the proprietor, gave up his keys, and scampered away.

•    •    •    •    •    •

And now on the Rue de la Victoire stands the abandoned house, "The Accursed House," whose history I have told you. Dust thickens upon the closed slats, grass grows in the court. No tenant ever presents himself now; and in the quarter, where stands this Accursed House, so funereal is its reputation that even the neighboring houses on either side of it have also depreciated in value.

Lower one's rent!! Who would think of such a thing!!!

# "TO MAKE A HOOSIER HOLIDAY"

## By George Ade

If you will take a map of the State of Indiana
and follow with your pencil one of the many rail-
way lines radiating from Indianapolis, you will find,
if you are extremely diligent in your search, a black
speck marked "Musselwhite." It is not an asterisk,
meaning a county seat—simply a speck on the enam-
eled surface. Furthermore, it is one of many specks.
A map which shows all of the towns of the Musselwhite kind looks like a platter of caviare—a mere
scramble of dark globules, each the same as the
others.

As a matter of fact, Musselwhite seemed one of
a thousand to the sleepy travelers in the parlor cars.
Lying back on their upholstered griddles, slowly bak-
ing to a crisp, they would be aroused by a succession
of jolts and grinds and would look out with torpid
interest at a brindle-colored "depot," a few brick
stores ornately faced with cornices of galvanized iron,
a straggling row of frame houses, prigged out with
scallops and protuberant bay windows, a few alert
horses at the hitch-rack and a few somnolent Ameri-
cans punctuated along the platform. Then the train
would laboriously push this panorama into the background and whisk away into the cornfields, and the

(Reprinted, by permission of the author, from Collier's Weekly for
December 17, 1904; copyright, 1904, by P. F. Collier &
Son Co.)

travelers would never again think of Musselwhite.
Certainly they would never think of it as a hotbed
of politics, an arena of social strivings, a Mecca for
the remote farmhand and a headquarters for religious effort. Yet Musselwhite was all of these—and
more.

The town had two wings of the Protestant faith,
but they did not always flap in unison. They were
united in the single belief that the Catholic congregation at the other end of town was intent on
some dark plan to capture the government and blow
up the public school system.

The Zion Methodist Church stood across the street
from the Campbellite structure. Each had a high
wooden steeple and a clangorous bell. Zion Church
had an undersized pipe-organ which had to be pumped
from behind. The Campbellites had merely an over-
grown cottage organ, but they put in a cornet to
help out—this in the face of a protest from the conservative element that true religion did not harmonize
with any "brass-band trimmings."

In the Campbellite Church the rostrum was mov-
able, and underneath was a baptismal pool wherein
the newly converted were publicly immersed. Whenever there was to be a Sunday night "baptizing"
at the Campbellite Church, the attendance was over-
flowing. The Methodists could offer no ceremony
to compare with that of a bold descent into the cold
plunge, but every winter they had a "protracted
meeting" which kept the church lighted and warmed
for seven nights in the week. During this "revival"
period the Campbellites were in partial eclipse.

It must not be assumed that there was any petty
rivalry between the two flocks. It was the strong

and healthy competition between two laborers in the vineyard, each striving to pick the larger bunch of grapes. If the Zion Church gave a mush-and-milk sociable, it was only natural that the Campbellites, in their endeavor to retain a hold on the friendly sympathies of Musselwhite, should almost immediately make announcement of a rummage party or an old people's concert. The Campbellites had their Sunday school in the morning, preceding the regular service, and the Methodists had theirs in the afternoon. The attendance records and missionary collections were zealously compared. Unusual inducements were offered to the growing youth of Musselwhite to memorize the golden text and fight manfully for the large blue card which was the reward for unbroken attendance. In Musselwhite, as in many other communities, there were parents who believed in permitting the children to attend two religious services every Sunday, thereby establishing a good general average for the family, even if the parents remained at home to read the Sunday papers. The children found no fault with this arrangement. The morning Sunday school was a sort of full-dress rehearsal for the afternoon service, to which the children flocked in confident possession of those hidden meanings of the Scripture which can always be elucidated by a hardware merchant who wears dark clothes once a week.

At Christmas time the "scholars" found themselves in a quandary. Each church had exercises Christmas Eve. A child can not be in two places at the same time, no matter how busy his effort or how earnest his intention. And so it came about that the congregation offering the more spectacular entertainment and the larger portion of mixed candy drew the ma-

jority of the lambkins. The rivalry between the
Methodists and the Campbellites touched perihelion
on Christmas Eve. An ordinary Christmas tree
studded with tapers, festooned with popcorn, and
heavy with presents no longer satisfied the junior
population, for it had been pampered and fed upon
novelty. The children demanded a low-comedy Santa
Claus in a fur coat. They had to be given star parts
in cantatas, or else be permitted to speak "pieces"
in costume. One year the Campbellites varied the
program by having a scenic chimney-corner erected
back of the pulpit. There was an open fireplace glowing with imitation coals. In front of the fireplace
was a row of stockings, some of which were of most
mirth-provoking length and capacity, for the sense
of humor was rampant in Musselwhite. A murmur
of impatient and restless curiosity rather interfered
with the recitations and responsive readings which
opened the program. It rose to a tiptoe of eager
anticipation when Mr. Eugene Robinson, the Super-
intendent of the Sunday school, arose and, after a
few felicitous remarks, which called forth hysterical
laughter, read a telegram from Kriss Kringle saying
that he would arrive in Musselwhite at 8:30 sharp.
Almost immediately there was heard the jingle of
sleighbells. The older and more sophisticated boys
identified the tone as coming from a strand of bells
owned by Henry Boardman, who kept the livery barn,
but the minds of the younger brood were singularly
free from all doubt and questioning. A distinct
"Whoa!" was heard, and then the Saint, swaddled
in furs and with a most prodigious growth of cotton
whiskers, came right out through the fireplace with
his pack on his back and asked in a loud voice, "Is

this the town of Musselwhite?" His shaggy coat
was sifted with snow, in spite of the fact that the
night was rather warm and muggy, and his whole
appearance tallied so accurately with the pictures in
the books that the illusion was most convincing until
"Tad" Saulsbury, aged twelve, piped in a loud voice:
"I know who it is. It's Jake Francis."

His mother moved swiftly down the aisle and
"churned" him into silence, after which the distribution of presents proceeded with triumphant hilarity.

It was generally conceded that the Campbellite
chimney-corner entertainment rather laid over and
topped and threw into the shade any other Christmas
doings that had been witnessed in Musselwhite. That
is why the Methodists were spurred to unusual effort
one year later, and that is why "Doc" Silverton, Sam
Woodson, and Orville Hufty, as a special committee
on arrangements, met in the doctor's office one evening in November to devise ways and means.

"They're goin' to give another chimney-corner
show," said "Doc" Silverton. "We've got to do
something to offset it. I claim that the Christmas
tree is played out. Since they've started shippin' in
these evergreen trees from Chicago, a good many
people have their own trees right at home. We
can't very well take up the chimney-corner idee.
It's too much like trailin' along behind the Campbellites and takin' their dust."

"We've got to give 'em something new and different," said Orville Hufty. "I sent and got a book
that's supposed to tell how to get up shows for
Christmas, but it's all about singin' songs and speakin'
pieces, and we know by experience that such things
don't ketch the crowd here in Musselwhite."

"I've been thinkin'," said Sam Woodson, very slowly, "that we might do this: Go to the Campbellites and segest that we take turn about in givin' exhibitions. That is, if they hold off this year, we'll give them a clear field next year."

"Not much!" exclaimed "Doc" Silverton, with great decision. "That'd look like a clean backdown. Don't give 'em anything to crow about. Let's beat 'em at their own game. We can do it if you'll help me on a little scheme that I've been layin' awake nights and thinkin' about. Don't laugh when I tell you what it is. It's nothin' more or less than a weddin'."

"You mean to have somebody get married on Christmas Eve?" asked Mr. Hufty, looking at him coldly.

"That's it exactly," replied "Doc" with a grin of enthusiasm.

"What's gettin' married got to do with Christmas?" asked Sam Woodson.

"People get married every day," added Mr. Hufty.

"Not the people that I'm thinkin' about," said "Doc," leaning back and looking at them serenely. "Can you imagine what kind of a crowd we'll have in that church if we advertize that old 'Baz' Leonard is goin' to get married to Miss Wheatley?"

The other two committeemen gazed at "Doc" in sheer amazement, stunned by the audacity of his suggestion. "Baz" Leonard and Miss Wheatley! It took several moments for them to grasp the Napoleonic immensity of the proposition.

"Well, I'll be jiggered!" said Mr. Hufty. "How did you come to think of anything like that?"

"Is 'Baz' goin' to marry her?" asked Sam Woodson.

"He is," replied "Doc," but he don't know it— yet. I'm bankin' on the fact that he won't overlook a chance to show off in public, and that Miss Wheatley is about due to get married to some one."

"I think you'd be doin' her a favor if you picked out somebody besides 'Baz,'" suggested the cold and unresponsive Woodson.

"'Baz' is the man," said "Doc" firmly. "If we've got a public character in this town it's 'Baz' Leonard. If there's a woman in town that's supposed to be out of the marryin' class it's Miss Wheatley. Her gettin' married to any one would be about the biggest piece of news you could spring on Musselwhite. But gettin' married to 'Baz' Leonard! Say! They won't have a handful of people at their chimney-corner show. And you can bet they'll never keep Jake Francis over there to play Santa Claus. Any time that old 'Baz' gets married again, Jake'll want to be there to see it."

"I don't see how you're goin' to work it in on a Christmas Eve exhibition," said Woodson, but even as he spoke he chuckled reflectively, and it was evident that the beautiful possibilities of the plan were beginning to ramify his understanding.

"Simplest thing in the world," said "Doc." "We announce that we're goin' to give Miss Wheatley a Christmas present."

"You'd better postpone the show till April 1," suggested Mr. Hufty, and then all three committeemen leaned back in their chairs, exchanged glances, and roared with laughter. It was evident that no vote would be necessary.

"I've thought it all out," continued "Doc." "We can have the regular entertainment, then the distribution of presents. We'll have Santy Claus bring in the marriage license and present it to 'Baz.' Then we'll lead the happy couple to the altar, and after Brother

King has done a scientific job of splicin', we'll give them their combination Christmas and weddin' presents. The different Sunday school classes can chip in and buy presents for them. They'll be glad to do it."

"It sounds all right, but can we talk 'em into it?" asked Mr. Hufty. " 'Baz' has fooled around her a little, but I never thought he wanted to marry her."

"I'll guarantee to have him on hand when the time comes," said "Doc" confidently. "I want you two fellows to have the women go after Miss Wheatley. We must take it for granted that they're already engaged. Have the women go over and congratulate her, and then convince her that if she has a church weddin' she'll get a raft of presents. It's the third and last call with her, and I don't think we'll have to use blinkers or a curb bit."

And so, next day, there began the strangest campaign that ever Cupid waged by Proxy. Rumor—strong, persistent, undeniable—had it that "Baz" Leonard and Miss Beulah Wheatley were to become as one, indivisible. "United in the holy bonds of wedlock" is the way it was put by the editor of the "Courier."

Unless you, indulgent reader, have lived in a Musselwhite, you can not fully comprehend how convulsing was the excitement that laid hold upon the whole township when the story went jumping from house to house, across farm lots, over ditches, through the deep woods, until it was gleefully discussed around the lamplight as far away as Antioch and Burdett's Grove. For "Baz" Leonard was a man who had posed in the fierce light of publicity for many years. In Rome he would have been a senator. In Musselwhite he was a constable. As a war veteran, as a member of the Volunteer Fire Department, as a confirmed juror, as custodian of a bass drum, as judge of elections, as something-or-other, he contrived to be where the common run of mortals had to look at him and rather admire his self-possession and dignified bearing. To be in the foreground of activities, to be in some way connected with every event which partook of the ceremonial, this was the one gnawing ambition of Ballantyne Leonard. His front name, by some system of abbreviation known only to small towns, had been condensed to "Baz." His wife had died soon after the war. He lived in a small frame house, more thoroughly covered by mortgage than by paint. A pension and the occasional fee coming to a constable provided him with the essentials of life—tobacco and one or two other items less important. As a factor in the business life of Musselwhite he was a comparative cipher, but at public functions he shone. Take it on the Fourth of July. On a borrowed horse, with a tri-colored sash once around his waist and once over the shoulder, he led the parade. On election nights he read the returns. The job of pumping the organ in the Zion Church he refused because he could not perform his duties in view of the congregation. Every winter, when the Methodist revival had stirred the town to a high-strung fervor, he walked up the main aisle and joined the church, becoming for a few nights the nucleus of a shouting jubilation. Every summer he attended a soldiers' reunion, drank to the memory of blood-stained battlefields, and was let out of the church as a backslider. If a traveling magician or hypnotist requested "some one from the audience to kindly step upon the stage," "Baz" was always the first to respond. The happiness of his life came from

now and then being on a pedestal. "Doc" Silverton
knew what he was talking about when he said that on
Christmas Eve he would have his man on hand, ready
to be married.

As for Miss Beulah Wheatley, she was a small, prim,
and exceedingly antique maiden lady who looked out at
the world through a pair of bull's-eye spectacles.
Those whose memories extended back far enough
testified that, as a girl, she had been "not bad lookin',"
and they could account for her having been marooned
all these years only on the cruel theory that some
marry and some don't. Miss Wheatley was a pocket
edition of Joan of Arc when it came to church activities, her efforts being concentrated on foreign
missionary work. She was a landmark of Zion. "Doc"
Silverton once calculated that she had embroidered
twenty-seven pairs of slippers for the coming and going
preachers. It was known that she owned the house
in which she lived, and it was vaguely rumored that
she had money invested. In Musselwhite, flitting
about like a lonesome and unmated bird among
the satisfied and well-fed domestic pigeons, she was a
pathetic joke. People respected her because she was
pious and a good housekeeper, but likewise they poked
fun at her, for the "old maid" is always a fair target.

No two people in Musselwhite were more surprised
by the announced engagement than Mr. "Baz" Leonard
and Miss Beulah Wheatley. "Baz" met the first congratulations with good nature, his only sensation being
one of gratification that the public should be interested
in his private affairs. Later on, when his denials
were pooh-poohed into silence, and he was given
positive proof that Miss Wheatley had been up to
Babcock's store, picking out dress goods, he became

alarmed. Even this alarm was tempered by the joy of being the most-talked-about man in Musselwhite, and "Doc" Silverton never lost faith. At the first opportunity he called "Baz" into the office and gave him a long and violent handshaking. It's somethin' you ought to have done years ago, 'Baz,'" he said, leading his visitor over to an operating chair. "She's a fine woman, and she's got a little property, and I don't see that you could do better."

"I'd like to know how them reports got started," said "Baz." "I ain't seen Miss Wheatley for goin' on six weeks, and when I did see her we didn't talk about nothin' except them Plymouth Rock chickens she bought from—"

"That's all right, 'Baz,'" said "Doc," patting him on the shoulder. "You kept it quiet as long as you could, but Miss Wheatley's a woman, you know, and she was so proud of gettin' you away from all these widows around town, you can't blame her for braggin' a little. Now that it's all settled, we're going to give you the biggest weddin' that was ever seen in this neck of the woods."

Thereupon he outlined the plans for Christmas Eve, minimizing the fact that Miss Wheatley would be a party to the exercises, and enlarging upon the glory that would come to the groom. He told how the organ would thunder, how the church would be jammed, how the infant class would strew flowers in the pathway of the hero, and "Baz," listening, was lost.

In the meantime Mrs. Woodson and Mrs. Hufty had been working on Miss Wheatley. They did not falsify to her, but they led her to believe that Mr. Leonard had said many things that were really said by "Doc" Silverton, and they did it in such a way that the feminine conscience did not suffer a single pang. Miss Wheatley gathered, from the nature of their conversation, that they were the emissaries of the would-be groom. Certainly their assurances were emphatic, and she, as if in a dream, permitted herself to be measured for a wedding gown.

And so Miss Wheatley and "Baz" Leonard were engaged, and neither had spoken to the other a word that was even remotely suggestive of matrimony. "Doc" Silverton, past-master at politics and all manner of deep scheming, "clinched" the matter by giving a supper at the Commercial Hotel. "Baz" was present and Miss Wheatley was present and many witnesses were present. When the pie had been served, "Doc" arose and made a speech of congratulation to the couple. He referred to the undying splendor of Mr. Leonard's war record, his long and honorable career as a public servant, and the high esteem in which he was held by the beautiful little city of Musselwhite. It was meet and proper, said "Doc," that such a man should choose for his companion and helpmate an estimable lady whose light had never been hidden under a bushel, etc.

"Baz" and Miss Wheatley looked at each other across the celery tops, bewildered, but lacking the moral courage to arise and protest. They were being carried along on a wave of popular enthusiasm. It seemed exhilarating to Miss Wheatley. "Baz" wore an air of melancholy doubt, especially after the supper at the Commercial Hotel, when he had been given the privilege of taking a long, hard, and critical look at Miss Wheatley in her best clothes.

Word came to the committee that the groom was weakening. "Baz" had been meditating and gazing upon two pictures. One was pleasant—he at the church with a yellow rose in his coat and hundreds of people looking at him. The other was a long-drawn vista of straight and narrow matrimony under the supervision of a small but determined woman.

"I guess we'll have to call it off," he said, as he met "Doc" Silverton in front of the post-office, and he looked across the street in a guilty and shamefaced manner.

"You can't call it off," said "Doc." "You've announced your engagement in the presence of witnesses and we've fixed up the whole program."

"I didn't announce it—you did."

"Well, you were present, and silence gives consent. If you try to back out now she can sue you for breach of promise."

"What'll she git?"

"I'm surprised at you, 'Baz'—after all that your friends have done for you in this thing."

"Baz" studied a display of Christmas goods in a window and rubbed his chin reflectively. Finally he said, "I ain't got any clothes that's fit to wear."

"Doc" hesitated. The committee had not undertaken to outfit the bridegroom. But he knew that the failure of his pet enterprise would fill the town with Campbellite hilarity, so he said, "We'll see that you get a new suit."

Christmas Eve came. It found Musselwhite keyed up to the highest pitch of glad expectation. Every aspiring comic in the town had exhausted his stock of inventive humor in thinking up presents to give to "Baz" and Miss Wheatley. From cardboard mottoes of satirical character to a nickel-plated kitchen stove, the gifts, large and small, were waiting behind the pulpit of the Zion Church. As many people as could elbow their way into the seats and aisles and corners of the church were waiting. Miss Wheatley, all in white, with smelling salts, also six married women to give her courage, waited in the pastor's study. And down the street, in a small frame house, a grizzled veteran, who had faced death on many fields of carnage, lay back on his bed and told a despairing committee that he was ill, even to the point of death, and that there could be no wedding. He had put on the new black suit. The black bow tie had been carefully balanced by Sam Woodson. "Baz" with the dull horror of impending calamity numbing his resolution, had even combed his hair, and then, when Mr. Hufty looked at his watch and said, "It's about time to start," "Baz" had been stricken.

"Where does it seem to hurt you?" asked Sam Woodson.

"All over," said "Baz," looking steadfastly at the ceiling. "I'm as weak as a kitten."

"Your pulse is all right," said "Doc" Silverton, "and you've got a good color. Was Freeman Wheatley over to see you to-day?"

"Baz" rolled over and looked at the wall, and then answered hesitatingly, "Yes, I seen him for a little while."

"What did he say to you?"

"He said she didn't have as much property as most people think, and that no livin' man could get along with her."

"I thought you was slick enough to see through Freeman Wheatley," said Mr. Hufty. "He wants to sidetrack this thing so he'll come into her property."

"This is no time for foolin'," said "Doc" Silverton, arising and rolling up his sleeves. "There's nothin'

the matter with 'Baz' except he's a little overheated
by the pleasure of this gladsome occasion. I'll bleed
him and cool him off a little and he'll be all O. K."

Saying which he produced a pocket surgical case
and took out a long glittering knife.

"Don't you go to cuttin' into me," said "Baz,"
sitting up in the bed.

"Then you quit this tomfoolin' and come along with
us," said "Doc" sternly. "We ain't got a minute to
spare."

"Baz" thereupon showed immediate improvement.
With a deep sigh he stood up and they bundled him
into his overcoat.

The moonlit street was quite deserted. It seemed
that every one in town was waiting at the church.
"Doc" Silverton walked ahead with the silent victim.
Behind, Mr. Hufty and Sam Woodson executed quiet
dance steps in the snow, indicative of their joy.

In front of the Gridley house "Baz" stopped. "I
need a drink of water," he said. "I think it'd brace
me up."

"You can get one at the church," said "Doc."

'"I'd rather step in to the Gridley well here. It's
the best water in town."

The committee waited at the front gate. "Baz'
disappeared around the corner of the house and they
heard the dry clanking of the iron pump and the
splatter of water, and then there was silence and a
pause, but no "Baz" appeared.

"Mebbe he's slipped out the back way," suggested
Mr. Hufty in a frightened whisper, and the committee
ran for the pump. The Gridley back yard lay quiet
in the moonlight and there was neither sound nor
sight of bridegroom:

"He couldn't get away so soon," said "Doc." "I don't see any tracks in the snow."

"D'you s'pose—" began Sam Woodson, looking upward, and then he pointed to where Mr. "Baz" Leonard sat in the high crotch of a cherry tree.

"This is a put-up job," said Mr. Leonard. "I'm just gettin' on to it."

" 'Baz,' you're actin' like a child," began Mr. Hufty. "Come on, now; they're waitin' for you."

"Let him stay up there and freeze," said "Doc." "I'm done with him. I didn't think an old soldier would be afraid to face a crowd of people."

"I ain't afraid," said "Baz," shifting his position. "I've had the cards stacked on me, that's all."

"Go over to the church, Sam," said "Doc" Silverton, after an awkward pause. "Tell the whole crowd to come over here and take a look at the bridegroom that's gone to roost like a chicken." Sam started.

"Don't you bring no crowd here," shouted "Baz" as he began to descend. "This is the lowest trick that was ever put up on a human bein'."

Thus ended his resistance. They led him like a lamb to the slaughter.

People in Musselwhite said it was the making of "Baz" Leonard. For years after that he walked a chalk mark and his habits seemed to improve, for he was afraid to attend a soldiers' reunion. He should have been happy, for he lived in a cottage that was spick and span, and had a capable woman to tell him what to do at every turn. And yet there were times when, at Sunday morning services, he would look across at "Doc" Silverton with a reproachful light in his eyes, as if to say, "You did this to me."

# THE LADY OF LYONS, N. Y.

## By H. C. WITWER

She'll never look more beautiful than she did that
wild night when she stood beside me in Fairfax's
deadfall and told me to make good! I'll never be as
brainless again as I was that same evening when I let
her go with a paltry handshake. A fool and his money
is soon parted! Imagine a chilly good-by to the best
looker since Venus the Milo, when I might of cinched
matters then and there. I could of kissed her and she
wouldn't of shrieked, but it took me many a day to
find *that* part of it out. Well, when she told me to
leave Fairfax Falls flat on its collar bone and put myself over, she started something! Who was she? Wait
—I'm going to haul off and broadcast the low-down on
the whole business. This may not be as pungent as
Romeo & Juliet, but at least it's shorter.

Speaking of truffles, the first thing everybody usually
asks me is how did I ever manage to climb out of the
ash can and get to the top of the heap. I read the
other day where a great man was asked that same
question. "To what do you attribute your success?"
was the way it was put to him. They thought he was
going to say it was the influence of his mother, the
love of the little woman he was wed to, his early
religious training, working twenty-four hours a day, or
something like that. Well, he crossed 'em! "To what

(Copyright, 1926, by G. P. Putnam's Sons.)

do I attribute my success?" he says. "Why—to my *ability*, of course!"

There's a guy after my own heart—he had the courage not to be modest!

Altho I've yet to experience the sensations of being called anything else but Bill, not counting oaths, my rightful name is William R. Grimm, Esq. I graduated with high honors from the University of Experience and I'm entitled to place T. D. after my name if the mood should hit me. T. D. is a ten-letter vertical word meaning "Taxi Driver," and don't curl your lip— we can't all start life in Buckingham Palace. I guess you figure me hard-boiled. Well, if you'd been in hot water as much as *I* have, you'd be hard-boiled too!

That initial R in my name stands for the word Reginald and was a big concession on the part of my man-mountain father to my sainted and romantical mother, who, I understand, fondly wished to baptize me Percy. Dad was a roaring-voiced building contractor of the old two-fisted school—a handsome giant, from his pictures. Mother was his exact opposite— frail, dainty, refined. Their entirely different compositions has staged many a clash in *me!*

From my father I got my brawn and from my mother my ambition. Both parents was lost at sea when I was a kid, and the pennies which should of come to me was quickly dissipated by a equally dissipated uncle. It's certainly a crime that the only relations we can pick out for ourselves is our wives, ain't it?

Well, being thrown on my own at a age when I should of been a pupil in somebody's high school, my intentions has always been much better than my grammar. If they wasn't, I could be hung! I guess I've about covered the situation with regards to myself, except I might add that I never pick a fight and I never duck one. My motto is, "If hit on one cheek, turn the other—and if hit on the *other*, knock 'em cold!" Otherwise I'm polite to one and all, know my groceries, can wear a dress suit without somebody asking me to show them their table, read a lot to give myself a synthetic education and watch my speech like Puss watches a mouse. It ain't half as hard to come up from the gutter as it is to keep from bringing the gutter up with you. That last one's a *real* feat!

At the winsome age of twenty, which is where I'm going to begin giving you this load of my adventures, I was foiling the poorhouse by operating the only taxi in Fairfax Falls, N. Y. Husky, healthy, and not exactly resembling a gorilla, I didn't have a worry or a dime in the world. As I was still young enough to have dreams in the daytime, I firmly intended to check out of the taxi racket and win fame and fortune at *something*, but I hadn't located my trick as yet. Nevertheless, I'd made up my mind that some day a glass-paneled door was going to have on it in gold letters W. Reginald Grimm and underneath, President. Whether that would be followed by "Of the United States" or "Of the United Garbage Company," I didn't know or care!

I wasn't very fluent with money while I was bounding around at the wheel of a taxi, but I was certainly seeing a lot of life. What I missed in jack I made up in laughs! I also learned a lot of things which didn't do me no harm in later years—few people has as good a chance to view human nature as a taxi driver has. Experience is a hard school—no Yale or Harvard—but

for the pupils which will pay attention to Teacher it's
a great one!

My mock taxi, built by myself personally from
junked parts of a flock of different cars, was something
to think about. It cost me less than $150, and at that
price it was a steal. There was room enough for Con-
gress to meet in the thing and it had three speeds:
hither, thither, and yon. It would go anywheres—by
freight. Around Fairfax Falls they called it the Leap-
ing Tuna, but my name for it was the Gambler Six, as
it was nearly always broke. There was a garage in
this slab run by Skip Mullen who ground a mean valve,
but I done all my own repair work after one interview
with that baby. I asked him what I could do to stop
my motor from smoking, and he says to keep my
tobacco where the motor can't get at it! Skip writes
vaudeville acts for a living now. . . .

Left-Hook O'Brien and Butch Ford was my two best
pals in Fairfax Falls. In spite of the fact that we've
known each other for a dozen years now, by a strange
coincidence they're still my friends. O'Brien was a
classy lightweight box fighter and Butch was his trainer
and second—no drawing-room wows, but two of the
squarest shooters which ever put on a collar! Left-
Hook O'Brien was born Izzy Rabinowitz, but took that
Irish name for business purposes. He was nobody's
fool. Once when I kidded him about being a Jewish
Sinn Feiner, he grinned and answered me this:

"I like to have the crowd with me when I go in
there! Well, you listen to 'em the next time you see
a box fight. You'll hear 'Kill the Wop!' 'Knock the
Jew stiff!' 'Smack 'at Swede silly!' 'Flatten the big
Limey!' *But*—did you ever hear a fight crowd yell,
'Kill the *Irishman!*'?"

A pay-off, what?

O'Brien's one and only ambition was to cop the lightweight title, and Butch Ford's was to wake up every morning of his life with five bucks in his kick.

The first big turning point in my life arrived when Butch got me to drive him and Left-Hook O'Brien to Rochester, where O'Brien was to box Knockout Burns before going on to New York City for some more important quarrels. I'd seen O'Brien go a half dozen times before and I knew he was good, and so did the lightweight champion, which didn't wish no part of my boy friend. On paper, O'Brien figured to stop Knockout Burns in a couple of frames, and it looked like a great chance for me to win a few nickels for myself. Likewise, I'd see the brawl from a ring-side seat which Butch staked me to. As if that wasn't enough, business comes along and combines itself with the pleasure I looked forward to having. Just before I pulled out of town I got a call to stop at Lyons the day after the fight, pick up a school-teacher named Miss Baxter and haul her back to Fairfax Falls, where she was carded to do her stuff at our new schoolhouse.

Like everybody else, Left-Hook O'Brien rated Knockout Burns a push-over, and he trained for the battle by getting his nails manicured. At that, he give Burns a fearful pasting—made a chopping block of him—but he couldn't put him away. As game as a punching bag and as tough as a life sentence, Burns was in there to stay the limit. That's what he managed to do, tho in every round O'Brien done everything to this gil but run away with his wife! Burns being a local idol, the fair-minded referee called it a draw. If that scrimmage was a draw, so was the war! However, I bet that my buddy would slap Burns for a loop, and that rotten decision cost me my lifetime savings—thirty-four iron men. I had to borrow money for gas to get home on. Not so good!

Came the dawn, as they say on the screen, and right after a two-bit breakfast I shoved off for Lyons to get this school-teacher I was due to bring back to Fairfax Falls. On the way out of Rochester a female voice suddenly calls my name when I'm stopped by a traffic signal, and I immediately pull over to the curb, as the voice happens to belong to Pansy Pilkington. Don't laugh—Pansy's made many a wiser boy than me stop, look and listen! It was less than a year later that this palatable young lady was to stand New York on its head from the front row of the Follies. I know you never heard of no Pansy Pilkington in the Follies. Neither did nobody else. However, I ain't going to tip you the name she used there, as it's a hobby of mine to be a gentleman and Pansy was supposed to of hit Broadway direct from Vassar.

But at this time she was just a lowly biscuit shooter at the Commercial House in Fairfax Falls and probably thought Flo Ziegfeld was a ball player. The super-flapper of the burg and as soothing to the eye as green goggles, Pansy had that schoolgirl complexion without the bother of going to school. She was a disturbance of the first water, there's no question about that; still, she never made *me* feverish. I guess I was Pansy-proof. For one thing, I figured it would take too much Jack to step out with this Jill!

Her arms was full of bundles, and she dumped some on the front seat of my taxi beside me with a sigh of relief.

"Hello, Pansy," I says. "You look keen. How come you're in Rochester?"

"Well, Bill, I got sick of being a Mail-Order Mary!" she smiles. "You know—'send us only two dollars and get this beautiful Paris creation!' and 'Simply sign the coupon and the postman will toss this almost-fur in your door!' I've left that stuff to the Dumb Doras. I've been on a shopping carouse!"

"You wouldn't fool me, would you?" I grins back. "What did you use for money?"

"I love that!" says Pansy indignantly. "Suppose I told you I drew a month's salary in advance?"

"Be your age, Pansy," I says. "If you told *me* that, I'd get hysterical! That guy you work for ain't putting *nothing* out. He's too stingy to harbor a suspicion! Why——"

"Oh, that reminds me," butts in Pansy, opening her handbag excitedly, "to-day's the boss's birthday. Say —listen, Bill. Run over to that gents' furnishing store and pick out a nice tie for him—one you'd wear yourself. Here, this is all I have left!"

With that she hands me half a dollar.

"I can get him a collar for this, but not no tie," I says.

"But I have no more money," says Pansy, trying out some eye work on me. "Maybe *you*—er——"

"There ain't a chance of putting the bee on *me* either," I told her. "I'm as flat as a ballroom floor!"

And I explained to her what that Left-Hook O'Brien-Knockout Burns shambles done to me. Pansy looks vexed.

"Well, run over, anyways, and see what you can get for a man for fifty cents," she says. "I'll watch your taxi."

I prowled into this swell haberdashery, and they immediately suspected I wasn't by no means Vincent Astor, so they treated me accordingly.

"I want to get a tasty tie, and I got half a buck to squander," I tell a haughty clerk. "What would *you* suggest?"

The clerk gives me the up and down and yawns in my face. "I'd suggest another shop," he says and walks away.

A few doors above this drum there was a five-and-ten-cent store. I blowed in there and bought Pansy's boss *five* ties!

"I wish I could think of a little speech to make when I give him these," says Pansy.

"Just say, 'Here's some ties for your birthday—try and wear 'em!'" I says. "C'mon, hop in and I'll take you back home with me!"

I'd begun to think of the long voyage to Fairfax Falls with nothing for company but that school-teacher I had to get at Lyons—probably a comic valentine.

"I'd love to go back with you, Bill," says Pansy, "but—well, I have my return ticket and——"

"Here's a chance to play a mean trick on the railroad by not using it," I interrupts. "I got to pick up another lady at Lyons—she's going to teach at our new school—so you needn't be afraid to go with me."

"Afraid of *you?*" says Pansy, giving me a killing look. "Why, I'd never be afraid of *you*, Bill. I think you're a dear."

"I wouldn't be surprized," I says. "My father was a Elk!"

As a matter of fact, it was *me* which was afraid of Pansy.

"As for this school-teacher," continues Pansy, climb-

ing into the seat beside me and dumping her bundles
into the back of the cab, "let her *walk* to Fairfax Falls
or buy herself a pair of roller skates or something!"

But tho a long ride with just Pansy looked plenty
appetizing, I needed the sugar there was in it for me
if I took his school-teacher back, so I rolled into
Lyons, pulled up at the address I'd been given—and
got the shock of my young life!

Somehow I'd got the idea that this Miss Baxter
would be a hatchet-faced old maid as thin as a dime
and just as thrilling. I looked for horn-rimmed glasses,
hair plastered back flat, with a voice and costume about
like a man's. That's the way Miss Tice, our other
school-teacher, checked up—a girl which would be safe
anywheres, and I don't mean maybe!

Instead of that, Miss Baxter was simply a panic!
Around my own age, garbed in what Fairfax Falls
would be wearing about five years later, the latest bob,
the most recent everything else, a unbeatable argument
for short skirts—well, a breath taker! She just outclassed Pansy, which was anything but a eyesore herself.

Pansy looked three or four times as surprized as I
was, and she presented the Lady of Lyons with a
peeved stare. Pansy could of been in Finland as far as
Miss Baxter was concerned.

"I've been waiting an hour for you," this remarkable
and highly annoyed school-teacher says to me.

"Listen!" I says, somewhat dazed. "Don't get mad
over that hour's wait—*I* been waiting twenty years
for *you!*"

Pansy's scornful snort didn't stop us looking at each
other for maybe half a minute, during which Miss
Baxter executed a blush which ruined me. Then with

a quick frown she discouraged any further efforts on
my part, but as I hopped out and swung open the door
of the cab for her, her eyes was smiling if her lips
wasn't. With a murderous glance at me, Pansy got off
the front seat and stepped in the back too. She was
what you might call fuming. I introduced her to Miss
Baxter and explained how I happened to go out on a
call carrying a girl with me. Inwardly I was wishing
Pansy was in Portugal, not that I disliked her, but . . .
However, Miss Baxter seemed satisfied with my explanation and made room for Pansy beside her.

Then begun a ride to Fairfax Falls, which to me was
a riot, no kidding! Here I am with two beautiful girls
and a twenty-five-mile drive staring me in the face and
the fact that they're *both* there makes it out of the
question for me to click with one or the other. It was
a typical case of how happy I could be with either, was
the other dear charmer away!

In the back of the cab the girls is breaking their
necks to be polite to each other, but conversation died
a natural death after a few minutes and they didn't
even attempt to fake it. However, I was goaled by
Miss Baxter—Barbara Baxter, as I managed to eaves-
drop—and I took a noble try at promoting myself. I
managed to exchange some careless words with her
which soon steamed Pansy and caused that young lady
to high-hat me. This seemed to give Barbara much
secret amusement, and I guess that's the only reason
she talked to me at all. She must of thought I was a
fearful Patsy, then.

I got so interested in Barbara that I made a wrong
turn on a detour and lost the state road. So I stopped
outside a garage.

"What's the best way for us to get to Fairfax Falls from here?" I asked the near-mechanic which come out in answer to the horn.

This clown walks all around my home-made taxi, looking at it like it was the first one he ever seen in his born days.

"You wish to go to Fairfax Falls in *that* boiler?" he inquires, like he can't believe his ears.

"Absolutely," I says. "How will I get there?"

"Well, if it was *me,* I'd pray for a miracle!" he answers, curling his lip. With that he walks into the garage and both them girls laughed their heads off.

But I found the road, and no further noteworthy events happened till we're within a few miles of Fairfax Falls. Then it was different. The old boat is rattling off a noble twenty-five miles a hour when the sudden, hair-raising wail of a siren makes the girls jump. Through the rear-view mirror I peg a big, costly speed wagon, cut along racing lines, roaring over the road behind me. I recognized the car and I likewise knew that the proprietor of same had no right to use that siren, as he was neither a police car, a fire engine or a ambulance. I started to tell the nervous girls that, when this bozo, doing fifty mile a hour if he was moving at all, crowds me on a turn and we go crashing into a ditch with Pansy yelling murder. I still remember there wasn't a single squawk come from Barbara Baxter—she was a thoroughbred, that's positive!

However, we landed right side up and there was nobody hurt but my mudguards and temper. While I'm taking stock of the grief, our opponent drives slowly back around the turn, stops beside us, and gets out of his car. He was no stranger to me, being no

less than Jack Fairfax, the sheik of Fairfax Falls and
the first villain I ever met with a name like a hero.

Roughly about the same age, me and Fairfax has
been first-class enemies of years standing, our private
war starting long before when I knocked this tomato
stiff for deliberately running his car over my dog.

That's the tip-off on the kind of a guy he was—one
of these babies with a chin you love to touch!

Jack Fairfax was something of a mystery in our
town, where, in spite of the fact that it was named
after his family, he was as popular as typhoid fever.
His people had lived in Europe for years, and Fairfax
himself aced around mostly in Rochester and New
York City, tho nearly all Fairfax Falls was owned
by his parents. He simply drove in every now and
then to burn the natives up by Ritzing 'em, while
showing some of his rich, sarcastical, cake-eating
friends the village named after him.

Amongst the Fairfax properties was a crumbling old
mansion on the outskirts of the town which some time
before had been spread all over the Sunday magazine
sections of the newspapers as a haunted house. It was
still looked on that way by most of Fairfax Falls, and
the citizens give it a wide berth in passing by. You
couldn't get a kid within a mile of it! Strange noises,
clanking chains, unearthly lights and weird groans was
just a few of the "spirit signs" which half the town
swore to and the other half laughed off. Personally, I
was what you might call neutral, but through the fact
that Jack Fairfax constantly visited the place and
bragged about doing it, I figured the haunted-house
thing was apple sauce.

Well, when Fairfax come back that day after running me into the ditch I was naturally fit to be tied,

but on account of Barbara Baxter being there I didn't smack him down. Regarding the subject of girls going wild over cave men—well, some do and some don't! I was taking no reckless chances. Dressed like a fashion plate, with a cigaret sticking out of his mouth from a long, gold holder, this proper Humpty Dumpty stood there sneering at me, and, of course, alongside of him I looked like a tramp.

"I'm going to complain to the authorities about that remarkable conveyance of yours, Grimm," he says, with a nasty grin. "It's a menace to navigation!"

Pansy laughed, but Barbara didn't. I seen her coldly sizing him up.

"You should be heartily ashamed of yourself!" bursts out Barbara warmly. "We might have been killed!"

It was then Fairfax lamped her for the first time. One amazed look at her floored him—you could see that in his very readable face. Off comes his swagger cap. It hadn't come off for Pansy.

"Don't think because you're still on your feet that I'll forget this, Fairfax!" I says. "If we was alone, I'd lay you like linoleum, you big false alarm!"

But he pays me not the faintest attention. He's all eyes for Barbara Baxter.

"I—why—I—I gave you the horn and I tried to avoid crowding you, but I—I was going too fast!" he stammers, talking directly to her. "I'm terribly sorry! Won't you let me take you the rest of the way into town?"

At that I dropped the jack I was getting ready to raise the front wheels with and stared from him to Barbara. I noticed Pansy staring at *me*, and her face was good and angry. Fairfax had everything I didn't have—clothes, class, money, a swell car, a great line of chatter. Regardless of the miles there was between 'em in every other way, Fairfax and Barbara belonged in the same drawing-rooms, that was a cinch. I was just a taxi driver—where did *I* rate any favors from her?

Barbara hesitated and looked thoughtfully at me, while Fairfax's hungry eyes never left her face. He was hanging on her answer like it was a matter of life or death. I felt pretty low. To me it *was*—a matter of life or death to my hopes!

"How long will it take you to make repairs?" Barbara asks me.

"Five minutes!" I says before the words was hardly out of her pretty mouth.

"You're crazy!" snorts Fairfax, and he pulls open the door of my taxi. "If you'll step out, Miss——"

"I shall wait—you needn't bother!" interrupts Barbara, with icicles on every word, and my heart tries to climb out through my ribs.

"Get away from that cab, and make it snappy!" I bawls at Fairfax, taking a step toward him.

He moved slowly away and I could swear there was a touch of contempt in Barbara's glance at him. He seen it too, but the ignored and enraged Pansy give him a out—enabled him to take the air without choosing me.

"You can ride *me* into town, Mr. Fairfax," says Pansy, and hopping out of my taxi she flounces into the front seat of Fairfax's bus.

Fairfax hadn't invited her and this boy scout wasn't particularly overjoyed at the idea of rolling into Fairfax Falls with the Commercial House waitress by his side, beautiful or not. However, he had no choice and he shot away with a grinding of gears and probably a grinding of teeth too. The last *I* got was a poisonous glare from Pansy.

"I'm sorry I ain't got some magazines or something in the car to amuse you," I said calmly to Barbara, when they'd gone in a cloud of dust, "because it's going to take me a good hour and lots of equally good luck to get this mechanical toy where it'll roll!"

A flash of alarm in her lovely face is quickly chased by anger.

"What do you mean?" she demands. "Why did you tell me you could repair it in five minutes?"

"I wouldn't fool you—it was because I wanted you to stay!" I says truthfully, opening up the hood and gazing at the motor. "You're having a romantical adventure—don't scream!"

Wam—what a furious stare I got for a minute! Then I grinned cheerfully at her and darned if she didn't grin back.

"Why didn't you go into town with Fairfax—that other fellow?" I asked her, while I'm puttering around.

She opens a little beauty bag she's carrying and powders the end of the most bewitching nose since Helen from Troy.

"I do not like his type," she says. "You seemed to know him well—who is he?"

Well, that was just the beginning of four hundred and eighty-six questions asked me by this toothsome young lady while I'm trying to get Mr. Motor to mote. She wanted to know all about Fairfax Falls, the natives, the Fairfax family history, etc., etc., and even etc. The haunted house particularly aroused her attention

and she made me promise to show her the place at my
earliest convenience. Then she dreamily begins brush-
ing the sleeve of her dress with her lily-white hand.

"And—Pansy?" she asks me, without looking up.
"Your sweetheart?"

"By no means," I grins. "I ain't got no sweethearts
—I'm just a boy which girls forget!"

That extracted a laugh from Barbara, a delightful
sound as she handled it.

"You're a most unusual—er—taxi driver!" she says.
"Tell me something about yourself."

Well, at last we'd struck a subject on which I was
well posted, and I certainly done it justice! During
the course of the next half hour I broadcasted.

Barbara Baxter didn't pitch right into her job as
school-teacher, but Jack Fairfax stayed in town and
pitched right into trying to put over a fast one. He
fairly swamped Barbara with flowers, candy, books,
auto-ride invitations or what have you? Then, to my
great astonishment and rage, this scissorbill begin to
get results. Twice she went out riding with him, which
got me red-headed and tickled Pansy silly.

After giving matters plenty of due consideration, I
decided to interview Barbara on the subject of Jack
Fairfax. I seen her trip into Yackley's drug store one
morning and stopping my comedy taxi outside I
strolled in after her. We sat down at the fountain and
I plied her with a chocolate soda.

"Where have you been keeping yourself?" she asks
me, watching my face in the mirror behind the counter.
"Long time no see!"

"That don't seem to of ruined your health," I says
gloomily. "If I was you, I wouldn't give this Fairfax

too much leeway. Fun's fun, but that bird's forever looking for the best of it and——"

"Just a moment!" she cuts me off, colder by fifty-four degrees than the ice cream in her glass. "I think you forget that you and I are but chance acquaintances, Bill. You're not my father, my brother, my guardian or my fiancé. I'm quite able to take care of myself—in *any* company."

Surprized and hurt, I leaped up off the stool.

"Good-by and excuse me!" I says.

Darn it, I could feel my face flaming as red as all the tomatoes in the world. She had gave me the razzberry, cold turkey! I started for the door, positive that there ain't no Santy Claus, but she called me back —in a far different tone of voice.

"Is your taxi engaged?" she smiled—and I'm in love all over again.

"No," I says. "And *I* ain't engaged either. I ain't even *going* with nobody."

"Then take me out and show me that haunted house you told me about," she commands. "And take that sullen look off your face. You know, you're really handsome when you smile, Bill."

"When *you* smile, the rest of 'em is just girls," I says and told the truth.

Well, I drove her out to Fairfax's alleged haunted house and once we got there I had a hard time getting her to leave. Altho she'd asked me a raft of questions about this trap before, that didn't stop her from asking me all about it again. I never seen nobody so curious! Did anybody else besides Fairfax ever visit the haunted house? When and how often is the ghostly noises heard? Had the place ever been offered for sale? Did Fairfax himself tell people it was haunted?

That's just a few of the things Barbara wanted to know and I give her as many details as I had in stock.

Fairfax heard about this trip we took—probably from Pansy Pilkington which saw us coming back—and he gnashed his teeth. The very next day he walks up to my stand outside the hotel and says his car's in the repair shop and he wants to engage my taxi for the afternoon. He acted so friendly I should of been suspicious, but instead I was thrown off my guard. So I met him at two o'clock as arranged, and he orders me to drive him to the Commercial House. Still I don't tumble. But when he comes outside with Barbara Baxter on his arm I like to fell off my seat!

"Just drive us around for a couple of hours," says Fairfax, grinning from ear to ear. "I'll tell you when to come back!"

Barbara looked amazed when she seen me—staring first at Fairfax and then back at me. I thought she was in on this attempt to humiliate me and I give her a frigid glare. Up goes her head with a toss.

"You don't mind driving us?" she asks me.

"Why should I?" I shot at her. "This is my business, ain't it?"

But within a hour I was three feet past infuriation at the cracks Fairfax was making about me from the back of the cab. I suddenly whirled my taxi off the road, shot through a gap in a fence and drove 'em madly across a newly plowed field, stepping on the gas and nearly bumping my passengers and my seagoing taxi apart! When later I come to a halt outside the Commercial House, I'm satisfied I'd of dropped dead if a look from Fairfax could of killed me.

"How much do I owe you, you infernal idiot?" he pants, crazy mad.

"Twenty-five bucks, you inveterate sap!" I says, and taking off my coat I begin to roll up my sleeves.

Barbara tried hard to keep a straight face and glare at me, but she must of thought of something funny because all at once she bust out laughing, winked at me behind Fairfax's back and skipped into the hotel. Fairfax gazed after her, glowered at me for a minute, muttered a baffled oath and practically hurled the twenty-five fish at me. In a way, that was a disappointment. I was hoping he'd want to battle—if he had, he'd of sure got service!

About a week after Barbara Baxter descended on Fairfax Falls, a couple of more strangers got off 84, the dilapidated spur-line train, and stepped into my cab. Right off the bat I got a kick when they asked to be hauled to the haunted house. They're a pair of mysterious-looking eggs, and one of 'em must of spoke out of turn somewheres, because he had a broken nose. While I'm trying to figure 'em out, the other guy says they're newspaper reporters from New York City and they're going to write up something new and startling about the haunted house, but they don't wish nobody in Fairfax Falls to know of 'em being there. The fellow with the bum smeller then shows me a twenty-dollar note, tears it across and gives me half of it, telling me I'll get the other half if I drive to the haunted house as fast as my bus can go and by some route which won't take 'em through the town. I left 'em outside, looking at the house.

When I get back to my stand, I go to brush out the cab and I find one of them jazzbos has forgot to take a portfolio with him. So once again I drive to the haunted house, but there's no sign of nobody around, and tho I thump and thump on the front door I can't get no answer. Going around to the rear of this old ruin, I get a attack of dumfoundment. Cuddled up against a window is no less than Barbara Baxter, plainly getting a earful of what's going on inside the house!

"Well, for weeping in public!" I gasps, "what are *you* doing here?"

You should of saw her jump.

"I—why—I—well—er—spiritualism is a hobby of mine, Bill," she says, recovering her wits and coming over to me. "I've been studying the haunted house—listening for the—er—ghosts and that sort of thing, you know!"

She winds up with a little laugh which sounded to me like it was forced. I must say she seemed anything but at ease.

"Well, there ain't no ghosts in there now!" I says. "There's a couple of guys——"

"Yes—who *are* they?" she butts in excitedly.

"I promised I wouldn't tell," I says, after a minute. I was thinking of something else. "Say, listen—when are you going to begin teaching school here?" I ask her.

That innocent question didn't seem to add nothing to her peace of mind. She give me a long, odd look.

"Very soon, now," she says. "I'll wait in your taxi and you can drive me back to town. I—I *walked* out here, you know. And—Bill, don't say a word to those men in there, or to *any* one, about my being here!"

While Barbara sat in the cab around in front I pounded on the back door of the house till the fellow with the caved-in beak answered, asking who I was through the door before he opened it. I gave him the portfolio and he's highly delighted, calling to his pal to see what they nearly lost. This little act of honesty on my part wins me ten bucks more and a order to call for 'em at eight the following night. It wasn't till I'd left Barbara at the hotel that the thought struck me, "How did them two guys get in that house when it's always locked?"

Driving to the haunted house a little before 8 P. M. the following day, as per my engagement, who should call to me from the sidewalk but Barbara Baxter. No sooner does she find out where I'm bound for than she insists on going with me. Well, I was in a fine predicament. She wanted to go, she was sure she'd see the "ghosts" at night, and if you ever witnessed this girl you'd get a idea of how hard it was to refuse her *anything!* So I took her with me on the front seat, just to see what would happen. I seen what would happen, I'll howl to the wide, wide world!

I parked a little distance from the haunted house at Barbara's request and left her there while I walked up, knocked, and was let inside. The first thing I noticed is that the hall is full of wooden boxes, piled high on top of each other. One of the reporters says to back my taxi around to the rear, as they wish to load the boxes in it. I asks him where are they going, and he says to Rochester.

"Nothing stirring!" I says firmly. "I wouldn't wheel that old bus of mine to Rochester at night on a bet. Besides, it would fall apart with all them boxes in it. What's in 'em?"

"Never mind what's in 'em!" says the guy with the broken nose shortly, "but there's seventy-five bucks in this for *you* if you tend to your knittin'!"

But I had a sudden, queer feeling that something was wrong. I thought of Barbara sitting outside alone in my taxi, and I commenced to back out the hall, when a door's flung open and Jack Fairfax stumbles headlong into the house! He ain't got no hat on, and his face is as white as a sheet. Personally I'm commencing to get a bit dizzy.

"What the—" begins one of the reporters.

"The state troopers are on their way here—we're sunk!" bawls Fairfax and then he catches sight of me, "What did you let *that* fellow in here for?" he howls. "He's the one who tipped them off!"

Fairfax stood in the background, panting and swearing at me, but the two reporters rushed me together. We are wrestling all over the place when the doors crash in and the house is swarming with state troopers. I never seen so many guns before in all my life, and the next thing we're all pinched, including your boy friend Bill Grimm.

One of the troopers caved in the lid of a box in the hall, and it turns out to be full of bottles. The bottles is full of booze. Good night! Things had indeed come to a pretty pass, and I seen the hoosegow staring me right in the face, when Barbara Baxter saunters in the now open door. Fairfax, held by a couple of husky troopers the same as I was, give a gasp and looked thoughtful when he seen her, but I was too dazed to gasp—the whole thing smacked of a nightmare to *me!*

The troopers seemed to know Barbara and give her respectful attention, while she gives me a pleasant and unanswered smile. Then she tells 'em to take their hands off me, as I'm as innocent as a very young baby. Not only that, she goes on, but I've helped her get the evidence that Jack Fairfax and the other two scofflaws is the master minds of a state-wide gang of common,

ordinary bootleggers.  They was no more newspaper
reporters than I'm a Siamese duke!

While the troopers is loading their cursing prey and
the boxes of hooch into the cars outside, Barbara leads
the way into the deserted front room of the house and
tells me things.  There was spirits in that haunted
house all right, but they was *"spiritus frumenti"!*  It
seems State Prohibition Enforcement Headquarters had
been tipped that whisky was being brought to Fairfax
Falls from Canada, taken to the alleged haunted house,
and "cut" before being sold throughout the state.  Barbara Baxter, a special revenue agent, was sent to our
town as a school-teacher to get Fairfax and his pals
with the goods.

"Hasn't it all been thrilling, Bill?" she asks me, with
her hand on my arm.  But I'm half sore—half disappointed.

"You've made me look like a squealer!" I says, "I
ain't infatuated with Jack Fairfax by no means, but
that ain't the way I'd of boxed him.  I fight in the
open, myself!"

"But you've done a splendid thing!" says Barbara,
tho she did blush.  "They were vicious lawbreakers,
Bill, and——"

"Why did you give *me* a run-around about being a
school-teacher?" I shut her off.  "I told you the *truth*
about myself!"

"Bill—I—I had to feel my way carefully," she says.
"I had to know I could trust you!"

"Well, do you trust me now?" I asked her.

"Indeed I do!" she whispers.  Again her hand
touches my arm, and them Alice blue eyes look deep
into mine.  Standing as close to her as that in the
pitch-dark room, I got more kick than there was in all

of Fairfax's booze. I had to put on the brakes—hard!

"Being a copper is no job for a girl!" I busts out. I *had* to say something!

"Oh, isn't it?" says Barbara. "Well, I made good, didn't I? Bill—bootleg whisky ruined my home! It killed my father and cost my brother a high executive position. I wish I could put every one of those murderers in jail for life! I—why are you so—so quiet?"

"I'm thinking that the only reason you were so nice to me at all was to get the dope on them guys!" I told her.

"Then you're thinking wrong!" she says softly. "I—I like you, Bill!"

That's where we should of went into a clinch, but she was alone in that dark room with me, and she trusted me. I didn't know how she'd take it, and I refused to gamble! I figured it would keep, so I just said "Thanks!" and shook her hand.

"Bill," says Barbara, "are you going to be a taxi chauffeur all your life?"

"What's the difference?" I says. "It's a honest trade, and there's good money in it! I——"

"Nonsense!" she butts in. "Why don't you get out of Fairfax Falls, get rid of that absurd automobile, and start doing something big? Get into something worth while and lay the foundation for your future before it's too late. Why, there must be dozens of things you can do that offer more possibilities than driving a taxicab in a small town."

I said nothing at all—I was busy thinking. Then I realized I still had hold of her hand, and I let it go. We went out to my taxi, and I drove her back to town, the trip being made mostly in silence, tho she sit beside me on the front seat. When we got to the

Commercial House she says she was going to New York City to stay with her aunt for a while, and when I merely give her a gloomy "Good-by!" she seemed peeved, for some reason. Then she give me her aunt's address and phone number, again telling me to leave Fairfax Falls, which was cramping my style, for bigger fields and bigger opportunities. I took it for granted she was walking right out of my life when she walked up the stairs of that hotel. I'll never take *nothing* for granted again!

Well, I followed Barbara Baxter's advice, and I did get out of Fairfax Falls for a bigger playgrounds. I went to New York City, and I drove a taxi there!

Now *you* tell one.

# THE FETE AT COQUEVILLE

## By Emile Zola

### Chapter I

Coqueville is a little village planted in a cleft in the rocks, two leagues from Grandport. A fine sandy beach stretches in front of the huts lodged half-way up in the side of the cliff like shells left there by the tide. As one climbs to the heights of Grandport, on the left the yellow sheet of sand can be very clearly seen to the west like a river of gold dust streaming from the gaping cleft in the rock; and with good eyes one can even distinguish the houses, whose tones of rust spot the rock and whose chimneys send up their bluish trails to the very crest of the great slope, streaking the sky. It is a deserted hole. Coqueville has never been able to attain to the figure of two hundred inhabitants. The gorge which opens into the sea, and on the threshold of which the village is planted, burrows into the earth by turns so abrupt and by descents so steep that it is almost impossible to pass there with wagons. It cuts off all communication and isolates the country so that one seems to be a hundred leagues from the neighboring hamlets. Moreover, the inhabitants have communication with Grandport only by water. Nearly all of them fishermen, living by the ocean, they carry their fish there every day in their barks. A great

(Copyright, 1907, by P. F. Collier & Son Co. Translated by L. G. Meyer.)

commission house, the firm of Dufeu, buys their fish
on contract. The father Dufeu has been dead some
years, but the widow Dufeu has continued the business;
she has simply engaged a clerk, M. Mouchel, a big
blond devil, charged with beating up the coast and
dealing with the fishermen. This M. Mouchel is the
sole link between Coqueville and the civilized world.

Coqueville merits a historian. It seems certain that
the village, in the night of time, was founded by the
Mahés; a family which happened to establish itself
there and which grew vigorous at the foot of the cliff.
These Mahés continued to prosper at first, marrying
continually among themselves, for during centuries one
finds none but Mahés there. Then under Louis XIII
appeared one Floche. No one knew too much of where
he came from. He married a Mahé, and from that
time a phenomenon was brought forth; the Floches in
their turn prospered and multiplied exceedingly, so that
they ended little by little in absorbing the Mahés,
whose numbers diminished until their fortune passed
entirely into the hands of the newcomers. Without
doubt, the Floches brought new blood, more vigorous
physical organs, a temperament which adapted itself
better to that hard condition of high wind and of high
sea. At any rate, they are to-day masters of Coqueville.

It can easily be understood that this displacement of
numbers and of riches was not accomplished without
terrible disturbances. The Mahés and the Floches de-
test each other. Between them is a hatred of centuries.
The Mahés in spite of their decline retain the pride of
ancient conquerors. After all they are the founders,
the ancestors. They speak with contempt of the first
Floche, a beggar, a vagabond picked up by them from

feelings of pity, and to have given away one of their daughters to whom was their eternal regret. This Floche, to hear them speak, had engendered nothing but a descent of libertines and thieves, who pass their nights in raising children and their days in coveting legacies. And there is not an insult they do not heap upon the powerful tribe of Floche, seized with that bitter rage of nobles, decimated, ruined, who see the spawn of the bourgeoisie master of their rents and of their château. The Floches, on their side, naturally have the insolence of those who triumph. They are in full possession, a thing to make them insolent. Full of contempt for the ancient race of the Mahés, they threaten to drive them from the village if they do not bow their heads. To them they are starvelings, who instead of draping themselves in their rags would do much better to mend them.

So Coqueville finds itself a prey to two fierce factions—something like one hundred and thirty inhabitants bent upon devouring the other fifty for the simple reason that they are the stronger.

The struggle between two great empires has no other history.

Among the quarrels which have lately upset Coqueville, they cite the famous enmity of the brothers, Fouasse and Tupain, and the ringing battles of the Rouget ménage. You must know that every inhabitant in former days received a surname, which has become to-day the regular name of the family; for it was difficult to distinguish one's self among the cross-breedings of the Mahés and the Floches. Rouget assuredly had an ancestor of fiery blood. As for Fouasse and Tupain, they were called thus without knowing why, many surnames having lost all rational meaning in

course of time. Well, old Françoise, a wanton of eighty
years who lived forever, had had Fouasse by a Mahé,
then becoming a widow, she remarried with a Floche
and brought forth Tupain. Hence the hatred of the
two brothers, made especially lively by the question of
inheritance. At the Rouget's they beat each other to
a jelly because Rouget accused his wife, Marie, of
being unfaithful to him for a Floche, the tall Brisemotte, a strong, dark man, on whom he had already
twice thrown himself with a knife, yelling that he would
rip open his belly. Rouget, a small, nervous man, was
a great spitfire.

But that which interested Coqueville most deeply was
neither the tantrums of Rouget nor the differences between Tupain and Fouasse. A great rumor circulated:
Delphin, a Mahé, a rascal of twenty years, dared to
love the beautiful Margot, the daughter of La Queue,
the richest of the Floches and chief man of the country.
This La Queue was, in truth, a considerable personage.
They called him La Queue because his father, in the
days of Louis Philippe, had been the last to tie up his
hair, with the obstinacy of old age that clings to the
fashions of its youth. Well, then, La Queue owned
one of the two large fishing smacks of Coqueville, the
"Zephir," by far the best, still quite new and sea-
worthy. The other big boat, the "Baleine," a rotten old
patache,* belonged to Rouget, whose sailors were Delphin and Fouasse, while La Queue took with him
Tupain and Brisemotte. These last had grown weary
of laughing contemptuously at the "Baleine"; a sabot,
they said, which would disappear some fine day under
the billows like a handful of mud. So when La Queue
learned that that ragamuffin of a Delphin, the froth

---

* Naval term signifying a rickety old concern.

of the "Baleine," allowed himself to go prowling around
his daughter, he delivered two sound whacks at Margot,
a trifle merely to warn her that she should never be the
wife of a Mahé.  As a result, Margot, furious, declared
that she would pass that pair of slaps on to Delphin
if he ever ventured to rub against her skirts.  It was
vexing to be boxed on the ears for a boy whom she had
never looked in the face!

Margot, at sixteen years strong as a man and handsome as a lady, had the reputation of being a scornful
person, very hard on lovers.  And from that, added to
the trifle of the two slaps, of the presumptuousness of
Delphin, and of the wrath of Margot, one ought easily
to comprehend the endless gossip of Coqueville.

Notwithstanding, certain persons said that Margot, at
bottom, was not so very furious at sight of Delphin
circling around her.  This Delphin was a little blonde,
with skin bronzed by the sea-glare, and with a mane
of curly hair that fell over his eyes and in his neck.
And very powerful despite his slight figure; quite
capable of thrashing any one three times his size.
They said that at times he ran away and passed the
night in Grandport.  That gave him the reputation of
a werwolf with the girls, who accused him, among
themselves, of "making a life of it"—a vague expression in which they included all sorts of unknown
pleasures.  Margot, when she spoke of Delphin, be-
trayed too much feeling.  He, smiling with an artful
air, looked at her with eyes half shut and glittering,
without troubling himself the least in the world over
her scorn or her transports of passion.  He passed
before her door, he glided along by the bushes watching
for her hours at a time, full of the patience and the
cunning of a cat lying in wait for a tomtit; and when

suddenly she discovered him behind her skirts, so close to her at times that she guessed it by the warmth of his breath, he did not fly, he took on an air gentle and melancholy which left her abashed, stifled, not regaining her wrath until he was some distance away. Surely, if her father saw her he would smite her again. But she boasted in vain that Delphin would some day get that pair of slaps she had promised him; she never seized the moment to apply them when he was there; which made people say that she ought not to talk so much, since in the end she kept the slaps herself.

No one, however, supposed she could ever be Delphin's wife. In her case they saw the weakness of a coquet. As for a marriage between the most beggardly of the Mahés, a fellow who had not six shirts to set up housekeeping with, and the daughter of the mayor, the richest heiress of the Floches, it would seem simply monstrous.

Evil tongues insinuated that she could perfectly go with him all the same, but that she would certainly not marry him. A rich girl takes her pleasure as it suits her; only, if she has a head, she does not commit a folly. Finally all Coqueville interested itself in the matter, curious to know how things would turn out. Would Delphin get his two slaps? or else Margot, would she let herself be kissed on both cheeks in some hole in the cliff? They must see! There were some for the slaps and there were some for the kisses. Coqueville was in revolution.

In the village two people only, the curé and the *garde champêtre,** belonged neither to the Mahés nor to the Floches. The *garde champêtre,* a tall, dried-up fellow, whose name no one knew, but who was called

------
* Watchman.

the Emperor, no doubt because he had served under Charles X, as a matter of fact exercised no burdensome supervision over the commune which was all bare rocks and waste lands. A sub-prefect who patronized him had created for him the sinecure where he devoured in peace his very small living.

As for the Abbé Radiguet, he was one of those simple-minded priests whom the bishop, in his desire to be rid of him, buries in some out of the way hole. He lived the life of an honest man, once more turned peasant, hoeing his little garden redeemed from the rock, smoking his pipe and watching his salads grow. His sole fault was a gluttony which he knew not how to refine, reduced to adoring mackerel and to drinking, at times, more cider than he could contain. In other respects, the father of his parishioners, who came at long intervals to hear a mass to ⋅ lease him.

But the curé and the *garde champêtre* were obliged to take sides after having succeeded for a long time in remaining neutral. Now, the Emperor held for the Mahés, while the Abbé Radiguet supported the Floches. Hence complications. As the Emperor, from morning to night, lived like a bourgeois [citizen], and as he wearied of counting the boats which put out from Grandport, he took it upon himself to act as village police. Having become the partizan of the Mahés, through native instinct for the preservation of society, he sided with Fouasse against Tupain; he tried to catch the wife of Rouget in *flagrante delicto* with Brisemotte, and above all he closed his eyes when he saw Delphin slipping into Margot's courtyard. The worst of it was that these tactics brought about heated quarrels between the Emperor and his natural superior, the mayor La Queue. Respectful of discipline, the former heard the reproaches of the latter, then recommenced to act as his head dictated; which disorganized the public authority of Coqueville. One could not pass before the shed ornamented with the name of the town hall without being deafened by the noise of some dispute. On the other hand, the Abbé Radiguet rallied to the triumphant Floches, who loaded him with superb mackerel, secretly encouraged the resistance of Rouget's wife and threatened Margot with the flames of hell if she should ever allow Delphin to touch her with his finger. It was, to sum up, complete anarchy; the army in revolt against the civil power, religion making itself complaisant toward the pleasures of the bourgeoisie; a whole people, a hundred and eighty inhabitants, devouring each other in a hole, in face of the vast sea, and of the infinite sky.

Alone, in the midst of topsy-turvy Coqueville, Delphin preserved the laughter of a love-sick boy, who scorned the rest, provided Margot was for him. He followed her zigzags as one follows hares. Very wise, despite his simple look, he wanted the curé to marry them, so that his bliss might last forever.

One evening, in a byway where he was watching for her, Margot at last raised her hand. But she stopped, all red; for without waiting for the slap, he had seized the hand that threatened him and kissed it furiously. As she trembled, he said to her in a low voice: "I love you. Won't you have me?"

"Never!" she cried, in rebellion.

He shrugged his shoulders, then with an air, calm and tender, "Pray do not say that—we shall be very comfortable together, we two. You will see how nice it is."

## Chapter II

That Sunday the weather was appalling, one of those sudden calamities of September that unchain such fearful tempests on the rocky coast of Grandport. At nightfall Coqueville sighted a ship in distress driven by the wind. But the shadows deepened, they could not dream of rendering help. Since the evening before, the "Zéphir" and the "Baleine" had been moored in the little natural harbor situated at the left of the beach, between two walls of granite. Neither La Queue nor Rouget had dared to go out, the worst of it was that M. Mouchel, representing the Widow Dufeu, had taken the trouble to come in person that Saturday to promise them a reward if they would make a serious effort; fish was scarce, they were complaining at the markets. So, Sunday evening, going to bed under squalls of rain, Coqueville growled in a bad humor. It was the ever-lasting story: orders kept coming in while the sea guarded its fish. And all the village talked of the ship which they had seen passing in the hurricane, and which must assuredly by that time be sleeping at the bottom of the water. The next day, Monday, the sky was dark as ever. The sea, still high, raged without being able to calm itself, altho the wind was blowing less strong. It fell completely, but the waves kept up their furious motion. In spite of everything, the two boats went out in the afternoon. Toward four o'clock, the "Zéphir" came in again, having caught nothing. While the sailors, Tupain and Brisemotte, anchored in the little harbor, La Queue, exasperated, on the shore, shook his fist at the ocean. And M. Mouchel was waiting! Margot was there, with the half of Coqueville, watching the last surgings of the tempest, sharing her father's rancor against the sea and the sky.

"But where is the 'Baleine'?" demanded some one.

"Out there beyond the point," said La Queue. "If that carcass comes back whole to-day, it will be by a chance."

He was full of contempt. Then he informed them that it was good for the Mahés to risk their skins in that way; when one is not worth a sou, one may perish. As for him, he preferred to break his word to M. Mouchel.

In the meantime, Margot was examining the point of rocks behind which the "Baleine" was hidden.

"Father," she asked at last, "have they caught something?"

"They?" he cried. "Nothing at all."

He calmed himself and added more gently, seeing the Emperor, who was sneering at him:

"I do not know whether they have caught anything, but as they never do catch anything——"

"Perhaps, to-day, all the same, they have taken something," said the Emperor ill-naturedly. "Such things have been seen." La Queue was about to reply angrily. But the Abbé Radiguet, who came up, calmed him. From the porch of the church the abbé had happened to observe the "Baleine"; and the bark seemed to be giving chase to some big fish. This news greatly interested Coqueville. In the groups reunited on the shores there were Mahés and Floches, the former praying that the boat might come in with a miraculous catch, the others making vows that it might come in empty.

Margot, holding herself very straight, did not take

her eyes from the sea. "There they are!" said she simply.

And in fact a black dot showed itself beyond the point. All looked at it. One would have said a cork dancing on the water. The Emperor did not see even the black dot. One must be of Coqueville to recognize at that distance the "Baleine" and those who manned her.

"See!" said Margot, who had the best eyes of the coast, "it is Fouasse and Rouget who are rowing— The little one is standing up in the bow."

She called Delphin "the little one" so as not to mention his name. And from then on they followed the course of the bark, trying to account for her strange movements. As the curé said, she appeared to be giving chase to some great fish that might be fleeing before her. That seemed extraordinary. The Emperor pretended that their net was without doubt being carried away. But La Queue cried that they were do-nothings, and that they were just amusing themselves. Quite certain they were not fishing for seals! All the Floches made merry over that joke; while the Mahés, vexed, declared that Rouget was a fine fellow all the same, and that he was risking his skin while others at the least puff of wind preferred *terra firma*. The Abbé Radiguet was forced to interpose again for there were slaps in the air.

"What ails them?" said Margot abruptly. "They are off again!" They ceased menacing one another, and every eye searched the horizon. The "Baleine" was once more hidden behind the point. This time La Queue himself became uneasy. He could not account for such maneuvers. The fear that Rouget was really in a fair way to catch some fish threw him off his

mental balance. No one left the beach, altho there
was nothing strange to be seen. They stayed there
nearly two hours, they watched incessantly for the
bark, which appeared from time to time, then disappeared. It finished by not showing itself at all any
more. La Queue, enraged, breathing in his heart the
abominable wish, declared that she must have sunk;
and, as just at that moment Rouget's wife appeared
with Brisemotte, he looked at them both, sneering,
while he patted Tupain on the shoulder to console him
already for the death of his brother, Fouasse. But he
stopped laughing when he caught sight of his daughter
Margot, silent and looming, her eyes on the distance;
it was quite possibly for Delphin.

"What are you up to over there?" he scolded. "Be
off home with you! Mind, Margot!"

She did not stir. Then all at once: "Ah! there they
are!"

He gave a cry of surprize. Margot, with her good
eyes, swore that she no longer saw a soul in the bark;
neither Rouget, nor Fouasse, nor any one! The "Baleine," as if abandoned, ran before the wind, tacking
about every minute, rocking herself with a lazy air.

A west wind had fortunately risen and was driving
her toward the land, but with strange caprices which
tossed her to right and to left. Then all Coqueville
ran down to the shore. One half shouted to the other
half, there remained not a girl in the houses to look
after the soup. It was a catastrophe; something inexplicable, the strangeness of which completely turned
their heads. Marie, the wife of Rouget, after a moment's reflection, thought it her duty to burst into tears.
Tupain succeeded in merely carrying an air of affliction.
All the Mahés were in great distress, while the Floches

tried to appear conventional. Margot collapsed as if she had her legs broken.

"What are you up to again!" cried La Queue, who stumbled upon her.

"I am tired," she answered simply.

And she turned her face toward the sea, her cheeks between her hands, shading her eyes with the ends of her fingers, gazing fixedly at the bark rocking itself idly on the waves with the air of a good fellow who has drunk too much.

In the meanwhile suppositions were rife. Perhaps the three men had fallen into the water? Only, all three at a time, that seemed absurd. La Queue would have liked well to persuade them that the "Baleine" had gone to pieces like a rotten egg; but the boat still held the sea; they shrugged their shoulders. Then, as if the three men had actually perished, he remembered that he was Mayor and spoke of formalities.

"Leave off!" cried the Emperor. "Does one die in such a silly way?" "If they had fallen overboard, little Delphin would have been here by this!"

All Coqueville had to agree, Delphin swam like a herring. But where then could the three men be? They shouted: "I tell you, yes!"—"I tell you, no!"— "Too stupid!"—"Stupid yourself!" And matters came to the point of exchanging blows. The Abbé Radiguet was obliged to make an appeal for reconciliation, while the Emperor hustled the crowd about to establish order. Meanwhile, the bark, without haste, continued to dance before the world. It waltzed, seeming to mock at the people; the sea carried her in, making her salute the land in long rhythmic reverences. Surely it was a bark in a crazy fit. Margot, her cheeks between her hands, kept always gazing. A yawl had

just put out of the harbor to go to meet the "Baleine."
It was Brisemotte, who had exhibited that impatience,
as if he had been delayed in giving certainty to Rouget's wife. From that moment all Coqueville interested itself in the yawl. The voices rose higher:
"Well, does he see anything?" The "Baleine" advanced with her mysterious and mocking air. At last
they saw him draw himself up and look into the bark
that he had succeeded in taking in tow. All held their
breath. But, abruptly, he burst out laughing. That
was a surprize; what had he to be amused at?
"What is it? What have you got there?" they shouted
to him furiously.

He, without replying, laughed still louder. He made
gestures as if to say that they would see. Then having
fastened the "Baleine" to the yawl, he towed her
back. And an unlooked-for spectacle stunned Coqueville. In the bottom of the bark, the three men—
Rouget, Delphin, Fouasse—were beatifically stretched
out on their backs, snoring, with fists clenched, dead
drunk. In their midst was found a little cask stove in,
some full cask they had come across at sea and which
they had appreciated. Without doubt, it was very
good, for they had drunk it all save a liter's worth
which had leaked into the bark and which was mixed
with the sea water.

"Ah! the pig!" cried the wife of Rouget, brutally,
ceasing to whimper.

"Well, it's characteristic—their catch!" said La
Queue, who affected great disgust.

"Forsooth!" replied the Emperor, "they catch what
they can! They have at least caught a cask, while
others have not caught anything at all."

The Mayor shut up, greatly vexed. Coqueville

brayed. They understood now. When barks are intoxicated, they dance as men do; and that one, in
truth, had her belly full of liquor. Ah, the slut!
What a minx! She festooned over the ocean with
the air of a sot who could no longer recognize his
home. And Coqueville laughed, and fumed, the Mahés
found it funny, while the Floches found it disgusting.
They surrounded the "Baleine," they craned their
necks, they strained their eyes to see sleeping there by
three jolly dogs who were exposing the secret springs
of the jubilation, oblivious of the crowd hanging over
them. The abuse and the laughter troubled them but
little. Rouget did not hear his wife accuse him of
drinking up all they had; Fouasse did not feel the
stealthy kicks with which his brother Tupain rammed
his sides. As for Delphin, he was pretty, after he had
drunk, with his blond hair, his rosy face drowned in
bliss. Margot had gotten up, and silently, for the
present, she contemplated the little fellow with a hard
expression.

"Must put them to bed!" cried a voice.

But just then Delphin opened his eyes. He rolled
looks of rapture over the people. They questioned him
on all sides with an eagerness that dazed him somewhat, the more easily since he was still as drunk as a
thrush.

"Well! What?" he stuttered; "it was a little cask—
There is no fish. Therefore, we have caught a little
cask."

He did not get beyond that. To every sentence
he added simply: "It was very good!"

"But what was it in the cask?" they asked him
hotly.

"Ah! I don't know—it was very good."

By this time Coqueville was burning to know. Every one lowered their noses to the boat, sniffing vigorously. With one opinion, it smelt of liquor; only no one could guess what liquor. The Emperor, who flattered himself that he had drunk of everything that a man can drink, said that he would see. He solemnly took in the palm of his hand a little of the liquor that was swimming in the bottom of the bark. The crowd became all at once silent. They waited. But the Emperor, after sucking up a mouthful, shook his head as if still badly informed. He sucked twice, more and more embarrassed, with an air of uneasiness and surprize. And he was bound to confess:

"I do not know— It's strange— If there was no salt water in it, I would know, no doubt— My word of honor, it is very strange!"

They looked at him. They stood struck with awe before that which the Emperor himself did not venture to pronounce. Coqueville contemplated with respect the little empty cask.

"It was very good!" once more said Delphin, who seemed to be making game of the people. Then, indicating the sea with a comprehensive sweep, he added: "If you want some, there is more there—I saw them— little casks—little casks—little casks—"

And he rocked himself with the refrain which he kept singing, gazing tenderly at Margot. He had just caught sight of her. Furious, she made a motion as if to slap him; but he did not even close his eyes; he awaited the slap with an air of tenderness.

The Abbé Radiguet, puzzled by that unknown tipple, he, too, dipped his finger in the bark and sucked it. Like the Emperor, he shook his head: no, he was

not familiar with that, it was very extraordinary.
They agreed on but one point: the cask must have
been wreckage from the ship in distress, signaled Sunday evening. The English ships often carried to
Grandport such cargoes of liquor and fine wines.

Little by little the day faded and the people were
withdrawn into shadow. But La Queue remained absorbed, tormented by an idea which he no longer
expressed. He stopped, he listened a last time to Delphin, whom they were carrying along, and who was
repeating in his sing-song voice: "Little casks—little
casks—little casks—if you want some, there are more!"

## Chapter III

That night the weather changed completely. When
Coqueville awoke the following day an unclouded sun
was shining; the sea spread out without a wrinkle, like
a great piece of green satin. And it was warm, one
of those pale glows of autumn.

First of the village, La Queue had risen, still
clouded from the dreams of the night. He kept looking for a long time toward the sea, to the right, to the
left. At last, with a sour look, he said that he must
in any event satisfy M. Mouchel. And he went away
at once with Tupain and Brisemotte, threatening Margot to touch up her sides if she did not walk straight.
As the "Zéphir" left the harbor, and as he saw the
"Baleine" swinging heavily at her anchor, he cheered
up a little saying: "To-day, I guess, not a bit of it!
Blow out the candle, Jeanetton! those gentlemen have
gone to bed!"

And as soon as the "Zéphir" had reached the open

sea, La Queue cast his nets. After that he went to
visit his "jambins." The jambins are a kind of
elongated eel-pot in which they catch more, especially
lobsters and red gurnet. But in spite of the calm sea,
he did well to visit his jambins one by one. All were
empty; at the bottom of the last one, as if in mockery,
he found a little mackerel, which he threw back
angrily into the sea. It was fate; there were weeks
like that when the fish flouted Coqueville, and always
at a time when M. Mouchel had expressed a particular desire for them. When La Queue drew in his nets,
an hour later, he found nothing but a bunch of seaweed.
Straightway he swore, his fists clenched, raging so
much the more for the vast serenity of the ocean, lazy
and sleeping like a sheet of burnished silver under the
blue sky. The "Zéphir," without a waver, glided along
in gentle ease. La Queue decided to go in again, after
having cast his nets once more. In the afternoon he
came to see them, and he menaced God and the saints,
cursing in abominable words.

In the meanwhile, Rouget, Fouasse, and Delphin
kept on sleeping. They did not succeed in standing
up until the dinner hour. They recollected nothing,
they were conscious only of having been treated to
something extraordinary, something which they did not
understand. In the afternoon, as they were all three
down at the harbor, the Emperor tried to question
them concerning the liquor, now that they had recovered their senses. It was like, perhaps, eau-de-vie
with licorice-juice in it; or rather one might say
rum, sugared and burned. They said "Yes"; they said
"No." From their replies, the Emperor suspected
that it was ratafia; but he would not have sworn to
it. That day Rouget and his men had too many pains

in their sides to go a-fishing. Moreover, they knew
that La Queue had gone out without success that
morning, and they talked of waiting until the next day
before visiting their jambins. All three of them, seated
on blocks of stone, watched the tide come in, their
backs rounded, their mouths clammy, half-asleep.

But suddenly Delphin woke up; he jumped on to
the stone, his eyes on the distance, crying: "Look,
Boss, off there!"

"What?" asked Rouget, who stretched his limbs.

"A cask."

Rouget and Fouasse were at once on their feet,
their eyes gleaming, sweeping the horizon.

"Where is it, lad? Where is the cask?" repeated
the boss, greatly moved.

"Off there—to the left—that black spot."

The others saw nothing. Then Rouget swore an
oath. 'Nom de Dieu!"

He had just spotted the cask, big as a lentil on the
white water in a slanting ray of the setting sun. And
he ran to the "Baleine," followed by Delphin and
Fouasse, who darted forward tapping their backs with
their heels and making the pebbles roll.

The "Baleine" was just putting out from the harbor when the news that they saw a cask out at sea
was circulated in Coqueville. The children, the women,
began to run. They shouted: "A cask! a cask!"

"Do you see it? The current is driving it toward
Granport."

"Ah, yes! on the left—a cask! Come, quick!"

And Coqueville came; tumbling down from its
rock; the children arrived head over heels, while the
women picked up their skirts with both hands to

descend quickly. Soon the entire village was on the beach as on the night before.

Margot showed herself for an instant, then she ran back at full speed to the house, where she wished to forestall her father, who was discussing an official process with the Emperor. At last La Queue appeared. He was livid; he said to the *garde champêtre*: "Hold your peace! It's Rouget who has sent you here to beguile me. Well, then, he shall not got it. You'll see!"

When he saw the "Baleine," three hundred metres out, making with all her oars toward the black dot, rocking in the distance, his fury redoubled. And he shoved Tupain and Brisemotte into the "Zéphir," and he pulled out in turn, repeating: "No, they shall not have it; I'll die sooner!"

Then Coqueville had a fine spectacle; a mad race between "Zéphir" and the "Baleine." When the latter saw the first leave the harbor, she understood the danger, and shot off with all her speed. She may have been four hundred meters ahead; but the chances remained even, for the "Zéphir" was otherwise light and swift; so excitement was at its height on the beach. The Mahès and the Floches had instinctively formed into two groups, following eagerly the vicissitudes of the struggle, each upholding its own boat. At first the "Baleine" kept her advantage, but as soon as the "Zéphir" spread herself, they saw that she was gaining little by little. The "Baleine" made a supreme effort and succeeded for a few minutes in holding her distance. Then the "Zéphir" once more gained upon the "Baleine," came up with her at extraordinary speed. From that moment on, it was evident that the two barks would meet in the neighborhood of the cask.

Victory hung on a circumstance, on the slightest mishap.

"The 'Baleine'! The 'Baleine'!" cried the Mahès.

But they soon ceased shouting. When the "Baleine" was almost touching the cask, the "Zéphir," by a bold maneuver, managed to pass in front of her and throw the cask to the left, where La Queue harpooned it with a thrust of the boat-hook.

"The 'Zéphir'! the 'Zéphir'!" screamed the Floches.

And the Emperor, having spoken of foul play, big words were exchanged. Margot clapped her hands. The Abbé Radiguet came down with his breviary, made a profound remark which abruptly calmed the people, and then threw them into consternation.

"They will, perhaps, drink it all, these, too," he murmured with a melancholy air.

At sea, between the "Baleine" and the "Zéphir," a violent quarrel broke out. Rouget called La Queue a thief, while the latter called Rouget a good-for-nothing. The men even took up their oars to beat each other down, and the adventure lacked little of turning into a naval combat. More than this, they engaged to meet on land, showing their fists and threatening to disembowel each other as soon as they found each other again.

"The rascal!" grumbled Rouget. "You know, that cask is bigger than the one of yesterday. It's yellow, this one—it ought to be great." Then in accents of despair: "Let's go and see the jambins; there may very possibly be lobsters in them."

And the "Baleine" went on heavily to the left, steering toward the point.

In the "Zéphir," La Queue had to get in a passion in order to hold Tupain and Brisemotte from the cask.

The boat-hook, in smashing a hoop, had made a leaking for the red liquid, which the two men tasted from
the ends of their fingers and which they found ex-
quisite. One might easily drink a glass without its
producing much effect. But La Queue would not have
it. He caulked the cask and declared that the first
who sucked it should have a talk with him. On land,
they would see.

"Then," asked Tupain, sullenly, "are we going to
draw out the jambins?"

"Yes, right away; there is no hurry!" replied
La Queue.

He also gazed lovingly at the barrel. He felt his
limbs melt with longing to go in at once and taste
it. The fish bored him.

"Bah!" said he at the end of a silence. "Let's go
back, for it's late. We will return to-morrow." And
he was relaxing his fishing when he noticed another
cask at his right, this one very small, and which stood
on end, turning on itself like a top. That was the last
straw for the nets and the jambins. No one even
spoke of them any longer. The "Zéphir" gave chase
to the little barrel, which was caught very easily.

During this time a similar adventure overtook the
"Baleine." After Rouget had already visited five
jambins completely empty, Delphin, always on the
watch, cried out that he saw something. But it did
not have the appearance of a cask, it was too long.

"It's a beam," said Fouasse.

Rouget let fall his sixth jambin without drawing
it out of the water. "Let's go and see, all the same,"
said he.

As they advanced, they thought they recognized

at first a beam, a chest, the trunk of a tree. Then they gave a cry of joy.

It was a real cask, but a very queer cask, such as they had never seen before. One would have said a tube, bulging in the middle and closed at the two ends by a layer of plaster.

"Ah, that's comical!" cried Rouget, in rapture. "This one I want the Emperor to taste. Come, children, let's go in."

They all agreed not to touch it, and the "Baleine" returned to Coqueville at the same moment as the "Zéphir," in its turn, anchored in the little harbor. Not one inquisitive had left the beach. Cries of joy greeted that unexpected catch of three casks. The *gamins* hurled their caps into the air, while the women had at once gone on the run to look for glasses. It was decided to taste the liquid on the spot. The wreckage belonged to the village. Not one protest arose. Only they formed into two groups, the Mahés surrounded Rouget, the Floches would not let go of La Queue.

"Emperor, the first glass for you!" cried Rouget. "Tell us what it is."

The liquor was of a beautiful golden yellow. The *garde champêtre* raised his glass, looked at it, smelt it, then decided to drink.

"That comes from Holland," said he, after a long silence.

He did not give any other information. All the Mahés drank with deference. It was rather thick, and they stood surprized, for it tasted of flowers. The women found it very good. As for the men, they would have preferred less sugar. Nevertheless, at the bottom it ended by being strong at the third or fourth glass. The more they drank, the better they liked it. The men became jolly, the women grew funny.

But the Emperor, in spite of his recent quarrels with the Mayor, had gone to hang about the group of Floches.

The biggest cask gave out a dark-red liquor, while they drew from the smallest a liquid white as water from the rock; and it was this latter that was the stiffest, a regular pepper, something that skinned the tongue.

Not one of the Floches recognized it, neither the red nor the white.

There were, however, some wags there. It annoyed them to be regaling themselves without knowing over what.

"I say, Emperor, taste that for me!" said La Queue, thus taking the first step.

The Emperor, who had been waiting for the invitation, posed once more as connoisseur.

"As for the red," he said, "there is orange in that! And for the white," he declared, "that—that is excellent!"

They had to content themselves with these replies, for he shook his head with a knowing air, with the happy look of a man who has given satisfaction to the world.

The Abbé Radiguet, alone, did not seem convinced. As for him, he had the names on the tip of his tongue; and to thoroughly reassure himself, he drank small glasses, one after the other, repeating: "Wait, wait, I know what it is. In a moment I will tell you."

In the mean while, little by little, merriment grew in the group of the Mahés and the group of the Floches. The latter, particularly, laughed very loud because they had mixed the liquors, a thing that excited them the more. For the rest, the one and the other of the groups kept apart. They did not offer each other of their casks, they simply cast sympathetic glances, seized with the unavowed desire to taste their neighbor's liquor, which might possibly be better. The inimical brothers, Tupain and Fouasse, were in close proximity all the evening without showing their fists. It was remarked, also, that Roget and his wife drank from the same glass. As for Margot, she distributed the liquor among the Floches, and as she filled the glasses too full, and the liquor ran over her fingers, she kept sucking them continually, so well that, tho obeying her father who forbade her to drink, she became as fuddled as a girl in vintage time. It was not unbecoming to her; on the contrary, she got rosy all over, her eyes were like candles.

The sun set, the evening was like the softness of springtime. Coqueville had finished the casks and did not dream of going home to dine. They found themselves too comfortable on the beach. When it was pitch night, Margot, sitting apart, felt some one blowing on her neck. It was Delphin, very gay, walking on all fours, prowling behind her like a wolf. She repressed a cry so as not to awaken her father, who would have sent Delphin a kick in the back.

"Go away, imbecile!" she murmured, half angry, half laughing; "you will get yourself caught!"

## Chapter IV

The following day Coqueville, in rising, found the sun already high above the horizon. The air was softer still, a drowsy sea under a clear sky, one of

those times of laziness when it is so good to do nothing
It was a Wednesday. Until breakfast time, Coque-
ville rested from the fête of the previous evening.
Then they went down to the beach to see.

That Wednesday the fish, the Widow Dufeu, M.
Mouchel, all were forgotten. La Queue and Rouget
did not even speak of visiting their jambins. Toward
three o'clock they sighted some casks. Four of them
were dancing before the village. "The Zéphir" and the
"Beleine" went in chase; but as there was enough for
all, they disputed no longer. Each boat had its share.
At six o'clock, after having swept all over the little
gulf, Rouget and La Queue came in, each with three
casks. And the fête began again. The women had
brought down tables for convenience. They had
brought benches as well; they set up two cafés in the
open air, such as they had at Grandport. The Mahés
were on the left; the Floches on the right, still separated by a bar of sand. Nevertheless, that evening
the Emperor, who went from one group to the other,
carried his glasses full, so as to give every one a taste
of the six casks. At about nine o'clock they were
much gayer than the night before. The next day
Coqueville could never remember how it had gone to
bed.

Thursday the "Zéphir" and the "Beleine" caught
but four casks, two each, but they were enormous.
Friday the fishing was superb, undreamed of; there
were seven casks, three for Rouget and four for
La Queue. Coqueville was entering upon a golden
age. They never did anything any more. The fishermen working off the alcohol of the night before, slept
till noon. Then they strolled down to the beach and
interrogated the sea. Their sole anxiety was to know

what liquor the sea was going to bring them. They waited there for hours, their eyes strained; they raised shouts of joy when wreckage appeared.

The women and children, from the tops of the rocks, pointed with sweeping gestures even to the least bunch of seaweed rolled in by the waves. And, at all hours, the 'Zéphir" and the "Baleine" stood ready to leave. They put out, they beat the gulf, they fished for casks, as they had fished for tun; disdaining now the tame mackerel who capered about in the sun, and the lazy sole rocked on the foam of the water. Coqueville watched the fishing, dying of laughter on the sands. Then in the evening they drank the catch.

That which enraptured Coqueville was that the casks did not cease. When there were no more, there were still more! The ship that had been lost must truly have had a pretty cargo aboard; and Coqueville became egoist and merry, joked over the wrecked ship, a regular wine-cellar, enough to intoxicate all the fish of the ocean. Added to that, never did they catch two casks alike; they were of all shapes, of all sizes, of all colors. Then, in every cask there was a different liquor. So the Emperor was plunged into profound reveries; he who had drunk everything, he could identify nothing any more. La Queue declared that never had he seen such a cargo. The Abbé Radiguet guessed it was an order from some savage king, wishing to set up his wine-cellar. Coqueville, rocked in mysterious intoxication, no longer tried to understand.

The ladies preferred the "cream"; they had cream of moka, of cacao, of mint, of vanilla. Marie Rouget drank one night so much anisette that she was sick.

Margot and the other young ladies tapped the curaçao, the benedictine, the trappistine, the chartreuse. As to the cassis, it was reserved for the little children. Naturally the men rejoiced more when they caught cognacs, rums, gins, everything that burned the mouth. Then surprizes produced themselves. A cask of *raki* of Chio, flavored with mastic, stupefied Coqueville, which thought that it had fallen on a cask of essence of turpentine. All the same they drank it, for they must lose nothing; but they talked about it for a long time. Arrack from Batavia, Swedish eau-de-vie with cumin, tuica calugaresca from Rumania, silvowitz from Servia, all equally overturned every idea that Coqueville had of what one should endure. At heart they had a weakness for kümmel and kirschwasser, for liqueurs as pale as water and stiff enough to kill a man.

Heavens! was it possible so many good things had been invented! At Coqueville they had known nothing but eau-de-vie; and, moreover, not every one at that. So their imaginations finished in exultation; they arrived at a state of veritable worship, in face of that inexhaustible variety, for that which intoxicates. Oh! to get drunk every night on something new, on something one does not even know the name of! It seemed like a fairy-tale, a rain, a fountain, that would spout extraordinary liquids, all the distilled alcohols, perfumed with all the flowers and all the fruits of creation.

So then, Friday evening, there were seven casks on the beach! Coqueville did not leave the beach. They lived there, thanks to the mildness of the season. Never in September had they enjoyed so fine a week. The fête had lasted since Monday, and there was no reason why it should not last forever if Providence should continue to send them casks; for the Abbé Radiguet saw therein the hand of Providence. All business was suspended; what use drudging when pleasure came to them in their sleep? They were all bourgeois, bourgeois who were drinking expensive liquors without having to pay anything at the café. With hands in pocket, Coqueville basked in the sunshine waiting for the evening's spree. Moreover, it did not sober up; it enjoyed side by side the gaities of kümmel, of kirschwasser, of ratafia; in seven days they knew the wraths of gin, the tendernesses of curaçao, the laughter of cognac. And Coqueville remained as innocent as a new-born child, knowing nothing about anything, drinking with conviction that which the good Lord sent them.

It was on Friday that the Mahés and the Floches fraternized. They were very jolly that evening. Already, the evening before, distances had drawn nearer, the most intoxicated had trodden down the bar of sand which separated the two groups. There remained but one step to take. On the side of the Floches the four casks were emptying, while the Mahés were equally finishing their three little barrels; just three liqueurs which made the French flag; one blue, one white, and one red. The blue filled the Floches with jealousy, because a blue liqueur seemed to them something really supernatural. La Queue, grown good-natured since he had been drunk, advanced, a glass in his hand, feeling that he ought to take the first step as magistrate.

"See here, Rouget," he stuttered, "will you drink with me?"

"Willingly," replied Rouget, who was staggering under a feeling of tenderness.

And they fell upon each other's necks. Then they all wept, so great was their emotion. The Mahés and the Floches embraced, they who had been devouring one another for three centuries. The Abbé Radiguet, greatly touched, again spoke of the finger of God. They drank to each other in the three liqueurs, the blue, the white, and the red.

*"Vive la France!"* cried the Emperor.

The blue was worthless, the white of not much account, but the red was really a success. Then they tapped the casks of the Floches. Then they danced. As there was no band, some good-natured boys clapped their hands, whistling, which excited the girls. The fête became superb. The seven casks were placed in a row; each could choose that which he liked best. Those who had had enough stretched themselves out on the sands, where they slept for a while; and when they awoke they began again. Little by little the others spread the fun until they took up the whole beach. Right up to midnight they skipped in the open air. The sea had a soft sound, the stars shone in a deep sky, a sky of vast peace. It was the serenity of the infant ages enveloping the joy of a tribe of savages, intoxicated by their first cask of eau-de-vie.

Nevertheless, Coqueville went home to bed again. When there was nothing more left to drink, the Floches and the Mahés helped one another, carried one another, and ended by finding their beds again one way or another. On Saturday the fête lasted until nearly two o'clock in the morning. They had caught six casks, two of them enormous. Fouasse and Tupain almost fought. Tupain, who was wicked when drunk, talked of finishing his brother. But that quarrel disgusted every one, the Floches as well as the Mahés. Was it reasonable to keep on quarreling when the whole village was embracing? They forced the two brothers to drink together. They were sulky. The Emperor promised to watch them. Neither did the Rouget household get on well. When Marie had taken anisette she was prodigal in her attentions to Brisemotte, which Rouget could not behold with a calm eye, especially since having become sensitive, he also wished to be loved. The Abbé Radiguet, full of forbearance, did well in preaching forgiveness; they feared an accident.

"Bah!" said La Queue; "all will arrange itself. If the fishing is good to-morrow, you will see—Your health!"

However, La Queue himself was not yet perfect. He still kept his eye on Delphin and leveled kicks at him whenever he saw him approach Margot. The Emperor was indignant, for there was no common sense in preventing two young people from laughing. But La Queue always swore to kill his daughter sooner than give her to "the little one." Moreover, Margot would not be willing.

"Isn't it so? You are too proud," he cried. "Never would you marry a ragamuffin!"

"Never, papa!" answered Margot.

Saturday, Margot drank a great deal of sugary liqueur. No one had any idea of such sugar. As she was no longer on her guard, she soon found herself sitting close to the cask. She laughed, happy, in paradise; she saw stars, and it seemed to her that there was music within her, playing dance tunes. Then it was that Delphin slipped into the shadow of the casks. He took her hand; he asked: "Say, Margot, will you?"

She kept on smiling. Then she replied: "It is papa who will not."

"Oh! that's nothing," said the little one; "you know

the old ones never will—provided you are willing,
you." And he grew bold, he planted a kiss on her
neck. She bridled; shivers ran along her shoulders.
"Stop! You tickle me."

But she talked no more of giving him a slap. In
the first place, she was not able to, for her hands were
too weak. Then it seemed nice to her, those little
kisses on the neck. It was like the liqueur that
enervated her so deliciously. She ended by turning her
head and extending her chin, just like a cat.

"There!" she stammered, "there under the ear—
that tickles me. Oh! that is nice!"

They had both forgotten La Queue. Fortunately
the Emperor was on guard. He pointed them out to
the Abbé.

"Look there, Curé—it would be better to marry
them."

"Morals would gain thereby," declared the priest
sententiously.

And he charged himself with the matter for the
morrow. 'Twas he himself that would speak to La
Queue. Meanwhile La Queue had drunk so much that
the Emperor and the Curé were forced to carry him
home. On the way they tried to reason with him on
the subject of his daughter; but they could draw from
him nothing but growls. Behind them, in the untrou-
bled night, Delphin led Margot home.

The next day by four o'clock the "Zéphir" and the
"Baleine" had already caught seven casks. At six
o'clock the "Zéphir" caught two more. That made
nine.

Then Coqueville fêted Sunday. It was the seventh
day that it had been drunk. And the fête was complete—a fête such as no one had ever seen, and which

no one will ever see again. Speak of it in Lower
Normandy, and they will tell you with laughter, "Ah!
yes, the fête at Coqueville!"


## Chapter V

In the mean while, since the Tuesday, M. Mouchel
had been surprized at not seeing either Rouget or
La Queue arrive at Grandport. What the devil could
those fellows be doing? The sea was fine, the fishing
ought to be splendid. Very possibly they wished to
bring a whole load of soles and lobsters in all at
once. And he was patient until the Wednesday.

Wednesday, M. Mouchel was angry. You must
know that the Widow Dufeu was not a commodious
person. She was a woman who in a flash came to high
words. Altho he was a handsome fellow, blond and
powerful, he trembled before her, especially since he
had dreams of marrying her, always with little attentions, free to subdue her with a slap if he ever became
her master. Well, that Wednesday morning the
Widow Dufeu stormed, complaining that the bundles
were no longer forwarded, that the sea failed; and
she accused him of running after the girls of the
coast instead of busying himself with the whiting
and the mackerel which ought to be yielding in abun-
dance. M. Mouchel, vexed, fell back on Coqueville's
singular breach of honor. For a moment surprize
calmed the Widow Dufeu. What was Coqueville
dreaming about? Never had it so conducted itself
before. But she declared immediately that she had
nothing to do with Coqueville; that it was M. Mouchel's business to look into matters, that she should
take a partner if he allowed himself to be played with

again by the fishermen. In a word, much disquieted,
he sent Rouget and La Queue to the devil. Perhaps,
after all, they would come tomorrow.

The next day, Thursday, neither the one nor the
other appeared. Toward evening, M. Mouchel, desperate, climbed the rock to the left of Grandport, from
which one could see in the distance Coqueville, with
its yellow spot of beach. He gazed at it a long time.
The village had a tranquil look in the sun, light smoke
was rising from the chimneys; no doubt the women
were preparing the soup. M. Mouchel was satisfied
that Coqueville was still in its place, that a rock from
the cliff had not crushed it, and he understood less and
less. As he was about to descend again, he thought
he could make out two black points on the gulf; the
"Baleine" and the "Zéphir." After that he went back
to calm the Widow Dufeu. Coqueville was fishing.
The night passed. Friday was here. Still nothing of
Coqueville. M. Mouchel climbed to his rock more
than ten times. He was beginning to lose his head;
the Widow Dufeu behaved abominably to him, without his finding anything to reply. Coqueville was
always there, in the sun, warming itself like a lazy
lizard. Only, M. Mouchel saw no more smoke. The
village seemed dead. Had they all died in their holes?
On the beach, there was quite a movement, but that
might be seaweed rocked by the tide. Saturday, still
no one. The Widow Dufeu scolded no more; her
eyes were fixed, her lips white. M. Mouchel passed
two hours on the rock. A curiosity grew in him,
a purely personal need of accounting to himself for
the strange immobility of the village. The old walls
sleeping beatifically in the sun ended by worrying him.
His resolution was taken; he would set out that Mon-

day very early in the morning and try to get down there near nine o'clock.

It was not a promenade to go to Coqueville. M. Mouchel preferred to follow the route by land, in that way he would come upon the village without their expecting him. A wagon carried him as far as Robineux, where he left it under a shed, for it would not have been prudent to risk it in the middle of the gorge. And he set off bravely, having to make nearly seven kilometers over the most abominable of roads. The route was otherwise of a wild beauty; it descended by continual turns between two enormous ledges of rock, so narrow in places that three men could not walk abreast. Farther on it skirted the precipices; the gorge opened abruptly; and one caught glimpses of the sea, of immense blue horizons. But M. Mouchel was not in a state of mind to admire the landscape. He swore as the pebbles rolled under his feet. It was the fault of Coqueville, he promised to shake up those do-nothings well. But, in the meantime, he was approaching. All at once, in the turning at the last rock, he saw the twenty houses of the village hanging to the flank of the cliff.

Nine o'clock struck. One would have believed it June, so blue and warm was the sky; a superb season, limpid air, gilded by the dust of the sun, refreshed by the good smell of the sea. M. Mouchel entered the only street of the village, where he came very often; and as he passed before Rouget's house, he went in. The house was empty. Then he cast his eye toward Fouasse's—Tupain's—Brisemotte's. Not a soul; all the doors open, and no one in the rooms. What did it mean? A light chill began to creep over his flesh. Then he thought of the authorities. Certainly, the

Emperor would reassure him. But the Emperor's house was empty like the others. Even to the *garde champêtre*, there was failure! That village, silent and deserted, terrified him now. He ran to the Mayor's. There another surprise awaited him: the house was found in an abominable mess; they had not made the beds in three days; dirty dishes littered the place; chairs seemed to indicate a fight. His mind upset, dreaming of cataclysms, M. Mouchel determined to go on to the end, and he entered the church. No more curé than mayor. All the authorities, even religion itself had vanished. Coqueville abandoned, slept without a breath, without a dog, without a cat. Not even a fowl; the hens had taken themselves off. Nothing, a void, silence, a leaden sleep under the great blue sky.

Parbleu! It was no wonder that Coqueville brought no more fish! Coqueville had moved away. Coqueville was dead. He must notify the police. The mysterious catastrophe exalted M. Mouchel, when, with the idea of descending to the beach, he uttered a cry. In the midst of the sands, the whole population lay stretched. He thought of a general massacre. But the sonorous snores came to undeceive him. During the night of Sunday, Coqueville had feasted so late that it had found itself in absolute inability to go home to bed. So it had slept on the sand, just where it had fallen, around the nine casks, completely empty.

Yes, all Coqueville was snoring there; I hear the children, the women, the old people, and the men. Not one was on his feet. There were some on their stomachs, there were some on their backs; others held themselves *en chien de fusils*.* As one makes his

* Primed for the event.

bed so must one lie on it.   And the fellows found
themselves, happen what may, scattered in their drunk-
enness like a handful of leaves driven by the wind.
The men had rolled over, heads lower than heels.   It
was a scene full of good-fellowship; a dormitory in
the open air; honest family folk taking their ease; for
where there is care, there is no pleasure.

It was just at the new moon.   Conqueville, thinking
it had blown out its candle, had abandoned itself to the
darkness.   Then the day dawned; and now the sun was
flaming, a sun which fell perpendicularly on the
sleepers, powerless to make them open their eyelids.
They slept rudely, all their faces beaming with the
fine innocence of drunkards.   The hens at early morning must have strayed down to peck at the casks, for
they were drunk; they, too, sleeping on the sands.
There were also five cats and five dogs, their paws in
the air, drunk from licking the glasses glistening with
sugar.

For a moment M. Mouchel walked about among the
sleepers, taking care not to step on any of them.   He
understood, for at Grandport they, too, had received
casks from the wreck of the English ship.   All his
wrath left him.   What a touching and moral spectacle!
Coqueville reconciled, the Mahés and the Floches
sleeping together!   With the last glass the deadliest
enemies had embraced.   Tupain and Fouasse lay there
snoring, hand in hand, like brothers, incapable of
coming to dispute a legacy.   As to the Rouget household, it offered a still more amiable picture.   Marie
slept between Rouget and Brisemotte, as much as to
say that henceforth they were to live thus, happy,
all the three.

But one group especially exhibited a scene of family

tenderness.  It was Delphin and Margot; one on the
neck of the other, they slept cheek to cheek, their
lips still opened for a kiss.  At their feet the Emperor,
sleeping crosswise, guarded them.  Above them La
Queue snored like a father satisfied at having settled
his daughter, while the Abbé Radiguet, fallen there
like the others, with arms outspread, seemed to bless
them.  In her sleep Margot still extended her rosy
muzzle like an amorous cat who loves to have one
scratch her under the chin.

The fête ended with a marriage.  And M. Mouchel
himself later married the Widow Dufeu, whom he beat
to a jelly.  Speak of that in Lower Normandy, they
will tell you with a laugh, "Ah! yes, the fête at
Coqueville!"

# THE WIDOW'S CRUISE

## By Frank R. Stockton

The Widow Ducket lived in a small village about ten miles from the New Jersey seacoast. In this village she was born, here she had married and buried her husband, and here she expected somebody to bury her; but she was in no hurry for this, for she had scarcely reached middle age. She was a tall woman with no apparent fat in her composition, and full of activity both muscular and mental.

She rose at six o'clock in the morning, cooked breakfast, set the table, washed the dishes when the meal was over, milked, churned, swept, washed, ironed, worked in her little garden, attended to the flowers in the front yard and in the afternoon knitted and quilted and sewed, and after tea she either went to see her neighbors or had them come to see her. When it was really dark she lighted the lamp in her parlor and read for an hour, and if it happened to be one of Miss Mary Wilkins's books that she read she expressed doubts as to the realism of the characters therein described.

These doubts she expressed to Dorcas Networthy, who was a small, plump woman, with a solemn face, who had lived with the widow for many years and who had become her devoted disciple. Whatever the widow did, that also did Dorcas—not so well, for heart told

(From a "Story-Teller's Pack"; copyright, 1897, by Charles Scribner's Sons.)

her she could never expect to do that, but with a yearning anxiety to do everything as well as she could.

She rose at five minutes past six, and in a subsidiary way she helped to get the breakfast, to eat it, to wash up the dishes, to work in the garden, to quilt, to sew, to visit and receive, and no one could have tried harder than she did to keep awake when the widow read aloud in the evening.

All these things happened every day in the summer time, but in the winter the widow and Dorcas cleared the snow from their little front path instead of attending to the flowers, and in the evening they lighted a fire as well as a lamp in the parlor.

Sometimes, however, something different happened, but this was not often, only a few times in the year. One of the different things occurred when Mrs. Ducket and Dorcas were sitting on their little front porch one summer afternoon, one on the little bench on one side of the door, and the other on the little bench on the other side of the door, each waiting until she should hear the clock strike five, to prepare tea. But it was not yet a quarter to five when a one-horse wagon containing four men came slowly down the street. Dorcas first saw the wagon, and she instantly stopped knitting.

"Mercy on me!" she exclaimed. "Whoever those people are, they are strangers here, and they don't know where to stop, for they first go to one side of the street and then to the other."

The widow looked around sharply. "Humph!" said she. "Those men are sailormen. You might see that in a twinklin' of an eye. Sailormen always drive that way, because that is the way they sail ships. They first tack in one direction and then in another."

"Mr. Ducket didn't like the sea?" remarked Dorcas, for about the three hundredth time.

"No, he didn't," answered the widow, for about the two hundredth and fiftieth time, for there had been occasions when she thought Dorcas put this question inopportunely. "He hated it, and he was drowned in it through trustin' a sailorman, which I never did nor shall. Do you really believe those men are comin' here?"

"Upon my word I do!" said Dorcas, and her opinion was correct.

The wagon drew up in front of Mrs. Ducket's little white house, and the two women sat rigidly, their hands in their laps, staring at the man who drove.

This was an elderly personage with whitish hair, and under his chin a thin whitish beard, which waved in the gentle breeze and gave Dorcas the idea that his head was filled with hair which was leaking out from below.

"Is this the Widow Ducket's?" inquired this elderly man, in a strong, penetrating voice.

"That's my name," said the widow, and laying her knitting on the bench beside her, she went to the gate. Dorcas also laid her knitting on the bench beside her and went to the gate.

"I was told," said the elderly man, "at a house we touched at about a quarter of a mile back, that the Widow Ducket's was the only house in this village where there was any chance of me and my mates getting a meal. We are four sailors, and we are mak- ing from the bay over to Cuppertown, and that's eight miles ahead yet, and we are all pretty sharp set for something to eat."

"This is the place," said the widow, "and I do give meals if there is enough in the house and everything comes handy."

"Does everything come handy today?" said he.

"It does," said she, "and you can hitch your horse and come in; but I haven't got anything for him."

"Oh, that's all right," said the man, "we brought along stores for him, so we'll just make fast and then come in."

The two women hurried into the house in a state of bustling preparation, for the furnishing of this meal meant one dollar in cash.

The four mariners, all elderly men, descended from the wagon, each one scrambling with alacrity over a different wheel.

A box of broken ship-biscuit was brought out and put on the ground in front of the horse, who immediately set himself to eating with great satisfaction.

Tea was a little late that day, because there were six persons to provide for instead of two, but it was a good meal, and after the four seamen had washed their hands and faces at the pump in the back yard and had wiped them on two towels furnished by Dorcas, they all came in and sat down. Mrs. Ducket seated herself at the head of the table with the dignity proper to the mistress of the house, and Dorcas seated herself at the other end with the dignity proper to the disciple of the mistress. No service was necessary, for everything that was to be eaten or drunk was on the table.

When each of the elderly mariners had had as much bread and butter, quickly baked soda-biscuit, dried beef, cold ham, cold tongue, and preserved fruit of every variety known, as his storage capacity would permit, the mariner in command, Captain Bird, pushed back his chair, whereupon the other mariners pushed back their chairs.

"Madam," said Captain Bird, "we have all made a good meal, which didn't need to be no better nor more of it, and we're satisfied; but that horse out there has not had time to rest himself enough to go the eight miles that lie ahead of us, so, if it's all the same to you and this good lady, we'd like to sit on that front porch awhile and smoke our pipes. I was a-looking at that porch when I came in, and I bethought to myself what a rare good place it was to smoke a pipe in."

"There's pipes been smoked there," said the widow, rising, "and it can be done again. Inside the house I don't allow tobacco, but on the porch neither of us minds."

So the four captains betook themselves to the porch, two of them seating themselves on the little bench on one side of the door, and two of them on the little bench on the other side of the door, and lighted their pipes.

"Shall we clear off the table and wash up the dishes," said Dorcas, "or wait until they are gone?"

"We will wait until they are gone," said the widow, "for now that they are here we might as well have a bit of a chat with them. When a sailorman lights his pipe he is generally willin' to talk, but when he is eatin' you can't get a word out of him."

Without thinking it necessary to ask permission, for the house belonged to her, the Widow Ducket brought a chair and put it in the hall close to the open front door, and Dorcas brought another chair and seated herself by the side of the widow.

"Do all you sailormen belong down there at the bay?" asked Mrs. Ducket; thus the conversation began, and in a few minutes it had reached a point at which Captain Bird thought it proper to say that a great many strange things happen to seamen sailing on the sea which lands-people never dream of.

"Such as anything in particular?" asked the widow, at which remark Dorcas clasped her hands in expectancy.

At this question each of the mariners took his pipe from his mouth and gazed upon the floor in thought.

"There's a good many things strange happened to me and my mates at sea. Would you and that other lady like to hear any of them?" asked Captain Bird.

"We would like to hear them if they are true," said the widow.

"There's nothing happened to me and my mates that isn't true," said Captain Bird, "and there is something that once happened to me. I was on a whaling v'yage when a big sperm-whale, just as mad as a fiery bull, came at us, head on, and struck the ship at the stern with such tremendous force that his head crashed right through her timbers and he went nearly half his length into her hull. The hold was mostly filled with empty barrels, for we was just beginning our v'yage, and when he had made kindling-wood of these there was room enough for him. We all expected that it wouldn't take five minutes for the vessel to fill and go to the bottom, and we made ready to take to the boats; but it turned out we didn't need to take to no boats, for as fast as the water rushed into the hold of the ship, that whale drank it and squirted it up through the two blow-holes in the top of his head, and as there was an open hatchway just over his head, the water all went into the sea

S. S. X–6

again, and that whale kept working day and night pumping the water out until we beached the vessel on the island of Trinidad—the whale helping us wonderful on our way over by the powerful working of his tail, which, being outside in the water, acted like a propeller. I don't believe anything stranger than that ever happened to a whaling-ship."

"No," said the widow, "I don't believe anything ever did."

Captain Bird now looked at Captain Sanderson, and the latter took his pipe out of his mouth and said that in all his sailing around the world he had never known anything queerer than what happened to a big steamship he chanced to be on, which ran into an island in a fog. Everybody on board thought the ship was wrecked, but it had twin screws, and was going at such a tremendous speed that it turned the island entirely upside down and sailed over it, and he had heard tell that even now people sailing over the spot could look down into the water and see the roots of the trees and the cellars of the houses.

Captain Sanderson now put his pipe back into his mouth, and Captain Burress took out his pipe.

"I was once in an obelisk-ship," said he, "that used to trade regular between Egypt and New York, carrying obelisks. We had a big obelisk on board. The way they ship obelisks is to make a hole in the stern of the ship, and run the obelisk in, p'inted end foremost; and this obelisk filled up nearly the whole of that ship from stern to bow. We was about ten days out, and sailing afore a northeast gale with the engines at full speed, when suddenly we spied breakers ahead, and our captain saw we was about to run on a bank. Now if we hadn't had an obelisk on board we might have sailed over that bank, but the captain knew that with an obelisk on board we drew too much water for this, and that we'd be wrecked in about fifty-five seconds if something wasn't done quick. So he had to do something quick, and this is what he did:  He ordered all steam on, and drove slambang on that bank.  Just as he expected, we stopped so suddint that that big obelisk bounced for'ard, its p'inted end foremost, and went clean through the bow and shot out into the sea.  The minute it did that the vessel was so lightened that it rose in the water and we then steamed over the bank. There was one man knocked overboard by the shock when we struck, but as soon as we missed him we went back after him and we got him all right.  You see, when that obelisk went overboard, its butt-end, which was heaviest, went down first, and when it touched the bottom it just stood there, and as it was such a big obelisk there was about five and a half feet of it stuck out of the water.  The man who was knocked overboard, he just swam for that obelisk and he climbed up the hiryglyphics.  It was a mighty fine obelisk, and the Egyptians had cut their hiryglyphics good and deep, so that the man could get hand and foot hold; and when we got to him and took him off, he was sitting high and dry on the p'inted end of that obelisk.  It was a great pity about the obelisk, for it was a good obelisk, but as I never heard the company tried to raise it, I expect it is standing there yet."

Captain Burress now put his pipe back into his mouth and looked at Captain Jenkinson, who removed his pipe and said:

"The queerest thing that ever happened to me was about a shark.  We was off the Banks, and the time of year was July, and the ice was coming down, and we got in among a lot of it. Not far away, off our weather bow, there was a little iceberg which had such a queerness about it that the captain and three men went in a boat to look at it. The ice was mighty clear ice, and you could see almost through it, and right inside of it, not more than three feet above the water-line, and about two feet, or maybe twenty inches, inside the ice, was a whooping big shark, about fourteen feet long—a regular man-eater—frozen in there hard and fast. 'Bless my soul,' said the captain, 'this is a wonderful curiosity, and I'm going to git him out.' Just then one of the men said he saw that shark wink, but the captain wouldn't believe him, for he said that shark was frozen stiff and hard and couldn't wink. You see, the captain had his own idees about things, and he knew that whales was warm-blooded and would freeze if they was shut up in ice, but he forgot that sharks was not whales and that they're cold-blooded just like toads. And there is toads that has been shut up in rocks for thousands of years, and they stayed alive, no matter how cold the place was, because they was cold-blooded, and when the rocks was split, out hopped the frog. But, as I said before, the captain forgot sharks was cold-blooded, and he determined to get that one out.

"Now you both know, being housekeepers, that if you take a needle and drive it into a hunk of ice you can split it. The captain had a sail-needle with him, and so he drove it into the iceberg right alongside of the shark and split it. Now the minute he did it he knew that the man was right when he said he saw the shark wink, for it flopped out of that iceberg quicker nor a flash of lightning."

"What a happy fish he must have been!" ejaculated

Dorcas, forgetful of precedent, so great was her emotion.

"Yes," said Captain Jenkinson, "it was a happy fish enough, but it wasn't a happy captain. You see, that shark hadn't had anything to eat, perhaps for a thousand years, until the captain came along with his sail-needle."

"Surely you sailormen do see strange things," now said the widow, "and the strangest thing about them is that they are true."

"Yes, indeed," said Dorcas, "that is the most wonderful thing."

"You wouldn't suppose," said the Widow Ducket, glancing from one bench of mariners to the other, "that I have a sea-story to tell, but I have, and if you like I will tell it to you."

Captain Bird looked up a little surprised.

"We would like to hear it—indeed, we would, madam," said he.

"Ay, ay!" said Captain Burress, and the two other mariners nodded.

"It was a good while ago," she said, "when I was living on the shore near the head of the bay, that my husband was away and I was left alone in the house. One mornin' my sister-in-law, who lived on the other side of the bay, sent me word by a boy on a horse that she hadn't any oil in the house to fill the lamp that she always put in the window to light her husband home, who was a fisherman, and if I would send her some by the boy she would pay me back as soon as they bought oil. The boy said he would stop on his way home and take the oil to her, but he never did stop, or perhaps he never went back, and about five o'clock I began to get dreadfully worried, for I knew

if that lamp wasn't in my sister-in-law's window by
dark she might be a widow before midnight.  So I said
to myself, 'I've got to get that oil to her, no matter
what happens or how it's done.'  Of course I couldn't
tell what might happen, but there was only one way
it could be done, and that was for me to get into the
boat that was tied to the post down by the water, and
take it to her, for it was too far for me to walk around
by the head of the bay.  Now, the trouble was, I
didn't know no more about a boat and the managin'
ɒf it than any one of you sailormen knows about clear-
starchin'.  But there wasn't no use of thinkin' what I
knew and what I didn't know, for I had to take it to
her, and there was no way of doin' it except in that
boat.  So I filled a gallon can, for I thought I might
as well take enough while I was about it, and I went
down to the water and I unhitched that boat and I put
the oil-can into her, and then I got in, and off I started,
and when I was about a quarter of a mile from the
shore—"

"Madam," interrupted Captain Bird, "did you row
or—or was there a sail to the boat?"

The widow looked at the questioner for a moment.
"No," said she, "I didn't row.  I forgot to bring the
oars from the house; but it didn't matter, for I didn't
know how to use them, and if there had been a sail
I couldn't have put it up, for I didn't know how to
use it, either.  I used the rudder to make the boat
go.  The rudder was the only thing I knew anything
about.  I'd held a rudder when I was a little girl, and
I knew how to work it.  So I just took hold of the
handle of the rudder and turned it round and round,
and that made the boat go ahead, you know, and—"

"Madam!" exclaimed Captain Bird and the other elderly mariners took their pipes from their mouths.

"Yes, that is the way I did it," continued the widow, briskly. "Big steamships are made to go by a propeller turning round and round at their back ends, and I made the rudder work in the same way, and I got along very well, too, until suddenly, when I was about a quarter of a mile from the shore, a most terrible and awful storm arose. There must have been a typhoon or a cyclone out at sea, for the waves came up the bay bigger than houses, and when they got to the head of the bay they turned around and tried to get out to sea again. So in this way they continually met, and made the most awful and roarin' pilin' up of waves that ever was known.

"My little boat was pitched about as if it had been a feather in a breeze, and when the front part of it was cleavin' itself down into the water the hind part was stickin' up until the rudder whizzed around like a patent churn with no milk in it. The thunder began to roar and the lightnin' flashed, and three sea-gulls, so nearly frightened to death that they began to turn up the whites of their eyes, flew down and sat on one of the seats of the boat, forgettin' in that awful moment that man was their nat'ral enemy. I had a couple of biscuits in my pocket, because I had thought I might want a bite in crossin', and I crumpled up one of these and fed the poor creatures. Then I began to wonder what I was goin' to do, for things were gettin' awfuller and awfuller every instant, and the little boat was a-heavin' and a-pitchin' and a-rollin' and h'istin' itself up, first on one end then on the other, to such an extent that if I hadn't kept tight hold of the rudder-handle I'd slipped off the seat I was sittin' on.

"All of a sudden I remembered that oil in the can; but as I was puttin' my fingers on the cork my conscience smote me. 'Am I goin' to use this oil,' I said to myself, 'and let my sister-in-law's husband be wrecked for want of it?' And then I thought that he wouldn't want it all that night, and perhaps they would buy oil the next day, and so I poured out about a tumblerful of it on the water, and I can just tell you sailormen that you never saw anything act as prompt as that did. In three seconds, or perhaps five, the water all round me, for the distance of a small front yard, was just as flat as a table and as smooth as glass, and so invitin' in appearance that the three gulls jumped out of the boat and began to swim about on it, primin' their feathers and lookin' at themselves in the transparent depths, tho I must say that one of them made an awful face as he dipped his bill into the water and tasted kerosene.

"Now I had time to sit quiet in the midst of the placid space I had made for myself, and rest from workin' of the rudder. Truly it was a wonderful and marvelous thing to look at. The waves was roarin' and leapin' up all around me higher than the roof of this house, and sometimes their tops would reach over so that they nearly met and shut out all view of the stormy sky, which seemed as if it was bein' torn to pieces by blazin' lightnin',' while the thunder pealed so tremendous that it almost drowned the roar of the waves. Not only above and all around me was everything terrific and fearful, but even under me it was the same, for there was a big crack in the bottom of the boat as wide as my hand, and through this I could see down into the water beneath, and there was—"

"Madam!" ejaculated Captain Bird, the hand which

had been holding his pipe a few inches from his mouth now dropping to his knee; and at this motion the hands which held the pipes of the three other mariners dropped to their knees.

"Of course it sounds strange," continued the widow, "but I know that people can see down into clear water, and the water under me was clear, and the crack was wide enough for me to see through, and down under me was sharks and swordfishes and other horrible water creatures, which I had never seen before, all driven into the bay, I haven't a doubt, by the violence of the storm out at sea. The thought of my bein' upset and fallin' in among those monsters made my very blood run cold, and involuntary-like I began to turn the handle of the rudder, and in a moment I shot into a wall of ragin' sea-water that was towerin' around me. For a second I was fairly blinded and stunned, but I had the cork out of that oil-can in no time, and very soon—you'd scarcely believe it if I told you how soon—I had another placid mill-pond surroundin' of me. I sat there a-pantin' and fannin' with my straw hat, for you'd better believe I was flustered, and then I begun to think how long it would take me to make a line of mill-ponds clean across the head of the bay, and how much oil it would need, and whether I had enough. So I sat and calculated that if a tumblerful of oil would make a smooth place about seven yards across, which I would say was the width of the one I was in—which I calculated by a measure of my eye as to how many breadths of carpet it would take to cover it—and if the bay was two miles across betwixt our house and my sister-in-law's, and, altho I couldn't get the thing down to exact figures, I saw pretty soon that I wouldn't have oil enough to make a level cuttin' through all those mountainous billows, and besides, even if I had enough to take me across, what would be the good of goin' if there wasn't any oil left to fill my sister-in-law's lamp?

"While I was thinkin' and calculatin' a perfectly dreadful thing happened, which made me think if I didn't get out of this pretty soon I'd find myself in a mighty risky predicament. The oil-can, which I had forgotten to put the cork in, toppled over, and before I could grab it every drop of the oil ran into the hind part of the boat, where it was soaked up by a lot of dry dust that was there. No wonder my heart sank when I saw this. Glancin' wildly around me, as people will do when they are scared, I saw the smooth place I was in gettin' smaller and smaller, for the kerosene was evaporatin', as it will do even off woolen clothes if you give it time enough. The first pond I had come out of seemed to be covered up, and the great, towerin', throbbin' precipice of sea-water was a-closin' around me.

"Castin' down my eyes in despair, I happened to look through the crack in the bottom of the boat, and oh, what a blessed relief is was! Far down there everything was smooth and still, and I could see the sand on the bottom, as level and hard, no doubt, as it was on the beach. Suddenly the thought struck me that that bottom would give me the only chance I had of gettin' out of the frightful fix I was in. If I could fill that oil-can with air, and then puttin' it under my arm and takin' a long breath if I could drop down on that smooth bottom, I might run along toward shore, as far as I could, and then, when I felt my breath was givin' out, I could take a pull at the oil-can and take another run, and then take another pull and another run, and perhaps the can would hold air enough for me until I got near enough to shore to wade to dry land. To be sure, the sharks and other monsters were down there, but then they must have been awfully frightened, and perhaps they might not remember that man was their nat'ral enemy. Anyway, I thought it would be better to try the smooth water passage down there than stay and be swallowed up by the ragin' waves on top.

"So I blew the can full of air and corked it, and then I tore up some of the boards from the bottom of the boat so as to make a hole big enough for me to get through—and you sailormen needn't wriggle so when I say that, for you all know a divin'-bell hasn't any bottom at all and the water never comes in—and so when I got the hole big enough I took the oil-can under my arm, and was just about to slip down through it when I saw an awful turtle a-walkin' through the sand at the bottom. Now, I might trust sharks and sword-fishes and sea-serpents to be frightened and forget about their nat'ral enemies, but I never could trust a gray turtle as big as a cart, with a black neck a yard long, with yellow bags to its jaws, to forget anything or to remember anything. I'd as lieve get into a bath-tub with a live crab as to go down there. It wasn't of no use even so much as thinkin' of it, so I gave up that plan and didn't once look through that hole again."

"And what did you do, madam?" asked Captain Bird, who was regarding her with a face of stone.

"I used electricity," she said. "Now don't stare as if you had a shock of it. That's what I used. When I was younger than I was then, and sometimes visited friends in the city, we often amused ourselves by rubbing our feet on the carpet until we got ourselves so full of electricity that we could put up our fingers and light the gas. So I said to myself that if I could get full of electricity for the purpose of lightin' the gas I could get full of it for other purposes, and so, without losin' a moment, I set to work. I stood up on one of the seats, which was dry, and rubbed the bottoms of my shoes backward and forward on it with such violence and swiftness that they pretty soon got warm and I began fillin' with electricity, and when I was fully charged with it from my toes to the top of my head, I just sprang into the water and swam ashore. Of course I couldn't sink, bein' full of electricity."

Captain Bird heaved a long sigh and rose to his feet, whereupon the other mariners rose to their feet. "Madam," said Captain Bird, "what's to pay for the supper and—the rest of the entertainment?"

"The supper is twenty-five cents apiece," said the Widow Ducket, "and everything else is free, gratis."

Whereupon each mariner put his hand into his trousers pocket, pulled out a silver quarter, and handed it to the widow. Then, with four solemn "Good evenin's," they went out to the front gate.

"Cast off, Captain Jenkinson," said Captain Bird, "and you, Captain Burress, clew him up for'ard. You can stay in the bow, Captain Sanderson, and take the sheet-lines. I'll go aft."

All being ready, each of the elderly mariners clambered over a wheel, and having seated themselves, they prepared to lay their course for Cuppertown.

But just as they were about to start, Captain Jenkinson asked that they lay to a bit, and clambering down over his wheel, he reentered the front gate and went up to the door of the house, where the widow and Dorcas were still standing.

"Madam," said he, "I just came back to ask what became of your brother-in-law through his wife's not bein' able to put no light in the window?"

"The storm drove him ashore on our side of the bay," said she, "and the next mornin' he came up to our house, and I told him all that had happened to me. And when he took our boat and went home and told that story to his wife, she just packed up and went out West, and got divorced from him. And it served him right, too."

"Thank you, ma'am," said Captain Jenkinson, and going out of the gate, he clambered up over the wheel, and the wagon cleared for Cuppertown.

When the elderly mariners were gone, the Widow Ducket, still standing at the door, turned to Dorcas.

"Think of it!" she said. "To tell all that to me, in my own house! And after I had opened my one jar of brandied peaches, that I'd been keepin' for special company!"

"In your own house!" ejaculated Dorcas. "And not one of them brandied peaches left!"

The widow jingled the four quarters in her hand before she slipped them into her pocket.

"Anyway, Dorcas," she remarked, "I think we can now say we are square with all the world, and so let's go in and wash the dishes."

"Yes," said Dorcas, "we're square."

# THE REGALARS

## By Charles Brackett

"Say," said Mae Smythe to her husband, interrupting a paddock conference between him and Herb Twitchell and Sam Mockton, the black jockey, which she wasn't supposed to be in on, "you know I guess I've made Bee Bernheimer awful mad."

Le Roy Smythe knew that if Mae had something to say it was quicker to listen right off. "How's that?" he asked.

"Well, I stopped at Bee's box just now and they wasn't anyone there but her, and if the people next door coulda heard it wasn't their business, and I says, 'Bee, I got a letter from your sister Essie today. I thought you'd be glad to know she's got a awful good job at last—doing towels in a laundry.' Well, Bee gives me a look you'da thought I'd hit her."

Le Roy chuckled.

"I guess Essie wouldn't have a very long run in the Smart Set," he commented.

"Well, she's an awful good-hearted girl just the same," Mae insisted, "and say, I betcha Bee tries to cheese me now for fair. Honest, she thinks she's grand now. Remember how green she was that first summer she come up here? I bet she wouldn'ta knew they was such a thing as a race track if it hadn't been for us. Gimmie ten dollars, will y', Roy? I wanta play it on my pony."

(Copyright, 1927, by Charles Brackett.)

Mae never bet unless she had the money on her person. It scared her too much for fear she'd lose.

"Nope," Le Roy said. "We ain't none of us gonta play him. He's outclassed, and we ain't got no money to throw away."

"Aw," Mae protested. "I bet he can beat anything on the card. He ain't outclassed, is he, Sam?"

Sam Mockton's grin was noncommittal.

"Well, go tell the Bum goo-by," Herb suggested. "We got some things to say to Mock."

"Well, I don't see what," Mae protested. "You act like I was listening in on a lodge meeting."

"You wouldn't know nothing about it. Better go see that Waltie ain't letting the Bum hang himself."

Waltie was Sam Mockton's moron brother and the only other member of the Smythe-Twitchell racing establishment. He was able to hold Reliable Bum when no one else was available, and was given board and lodging and the honorary title of "Rubber" for that accomplishment.

Waltie was afraid of women, so when Mae approached the stable he darted away from it with a scramble and squeak. Mae took Reliable Bum's head in her arms. The Bum was not an affectionate horse, but he tolerated Mae, and she got a lot of comfort out of him.

"I guess the Bernheimers ain't got nothin' as sweet as you," she told him. "Not that that's saying much."

It was indeed remarkable that a man of Berny Bernheimer's acumen should have had thrust upon him as much frail horseflesh as Berny had acquired in his brief two years as owner. If Bee had been a Regalar, Mae thought with satisfaction, she would have been chastened and humiliated by knowing what a joke his purchases were on the track. Recently, however, Berny had hired a new trainer named Holley. There was an intolerable possibility that he would set things straight in the Bernheimer stables.

"I ain't gonta have a cent on you today," Mae apologized to the Bum, to distract her mind from the thought. "Ain't that terrible? You can just bet I'm gonta write my lawyers to see if they can't collect that back alimony from Vernon, tho. It'd come in awful handy if the boys is gonta hold out on me like this. I been hearing that Vernon's took up bootlegging and is doing real good."

Le Roy and Herb's conference with Mockton was brief.

"They ain't giving but eight on the Bum, and it'll pay you to wait. Dontcha slip up now."

"No, suh."

"You do what I told you," Herb asserted himself. "Hand him the whip. I've seen him stop dead still at one touch of it."

"I kin do it pulling," Mockton protested.

Herb hadn't much faith in Mockton's pulling powers.

"You hand him the whip," he repeated impressively. "That's the way to make that baby sulk."

Then Herb and Le Roy went for Mae.

Mockton obeyed directions, and the race started depressingly enough for Mae. She was watching it almost lackadaisically when she heard Herb groan out, "That damned Nigger's dropped the whip," and saw the cerise of Mockton's blouse push out from the mass. Then it was that she hopped to the bench and began to whoop.

The Bum kept ahead.

Excitement rendered Mac's face a pink slightly different from the rouge she wore. She tore the pink hat from her brass-bright hair and waved it. Her voice would have done credit to a Cunarder.

"Reliable Bum! *Reliable Bum!* OH, YOU REE-LIABLE BUM*!*"

"Will you choke her, for Gawd's sake?" Herb groaned at Roy from the corner of his mouth, his one interest being that as little attention as possible be paid to the Bum's performance.

The Bum had won by that time, however, and Mae turned her lung power to winsome badinage.

"You're a nice pair," she rallied her writhing companions. "I thought my pony wasn't gonna win! Why was you tellin' me not to have anything up? You got a mad on your momma?"

"Did you hear her?" Bee Bernheimer asked the Society Show Girl. "Ain't she too common for words?"

"She's just umpossible," that lady pronounced.

Le Roy tried to heel Mae's near foot.

"Will y'cut it out, Mae?" he implored.

"I will not cut it out. Didn't I pick out that pony when he was a little sickly colt? I gotta right to yell. Didja see him slide down that stretch? Mock was sawing away scart to death.'

Mae was treading dangerous ground; fortunately for her pedal extremities, she shifted.

"Maybe Bee Bernheimer wouldn't give a couple quarts of diamonds to have one of Berny's cripples totter into the money. I gotta go and kiss my pony."

So saying she stepped to the floor, and started busily down the steps. At the Bernheimer box she paused and repeated, "I gotta go and kiss my pony."

Bee Bernheimer had a little lip-sticked mouth. She curled it very tight.

"Oh, was that your horse?" she exclaimed. "Ain't that nice for you? I guess a little money'll come in handy from some things I've heard dropped."

"Yeah, that was mine," Mae answered. "Y'see, here it is on the program, up to the top. That's where they puts the owner's name. You wanta tell Berny about that, because if one of his should ever get as far around as the clubhouse I should think he'd wanta know it."

She moved on tingling from Bee's dart.

"Come in awful handy!" she repeated to herself. "I guess I can remember when Bee was so afraid sump'n'd be docked off her five a week she'd pretty near swallow her gum if anybody hollered 'cash.' I do wish I hada had sump'n up, tho. I coulda got myself a awful pretty present if Roy had just give me ten dollars."

Her fancy roamed among the things she might have done with her winnings. A fish-scale dress in an inconspicuous shade of bottle green, which glittered in the window of one of the Broadway shops, would probably have been her choice. She thought of it with lingering tributes. "A nawful pretty little dress! . . . A sweet pretty little dress!"

Le Roy and Herb, who had followed Mae down, waited until they were out of the crowd before they loosened their grief's corset of silence.

"Hot Goophie!" Roy spoke first. "Eight to one! And next time we ain't gonna be able to make out the odds with a field glass!"

"They'll add weight too!"

"And Mae hadda tell the world we was counting on the Bum's losing. Wouldn'cha think a girl has been around with a coupla regalars as long as her would

know they was some science to running a horse?
Wouldn'cha think she'd know they was some things you
don't wanta yell around?"

Usually one or the other of them stuck up for Mae,
but occasionally, as now, you couldn't tell which was
her husband.

Mae heard their doleful tones behind her, and pivot-
ing on her hips, said archly:

"What's the matter with you boys, anyhow?  It
ain't a penitentiary offense to have a horse in the money
to-day, is it?"

"You wanta remember they are some things about
this game you don't understand, Mae," Le Roy hinted
darkly.

"Winning this race is goin' to give a lotta people a
awful wrong idea about the Bum."  Herb stuck in a
bit of propaganda.  "He's just as likely as not to lose
every race up to then.  The Bum's like that."

Herb's prognostication held more than good for three
races.  In fact, Reliable Bum was so singularly backward in all of them that, despite Mockton's boasts of
prodigious skill and strength in making him so, both
Herb and Roy began to feel uneasy about him.  You
never could believe Mockton, anyway.

"Let's just see once," Roy suggested.  "Even if he
wasta win now everybody'd say you can't count on
him.  It wouldn't change the odds much."

There were also financial reasons for the experiment,
so Herb consented.

The men ventured fifty each and let Mae have up
ten.

Never under any conditions had the Bum run worse
than he did that afternoon.  Halfway around the track

he was almost trodden underfoot by Gilt Girl, a filly of the Bernheimers', limping the course in bandages up to her knees.

"I guess you picked a bird dog when you picked the Bum, Mae," Herb remarked on their gloomy way home. "I wonder if we'd oughta run him in the Commercial atall. If he wasta put his head between his front legs and have a good cry like it looked like he was gonta once this afternoon, we'd haveta walk awful fast to keep the frost off our feet."

"You just wait and see," Mae said, in the unreasonable faith of her infatuation for Reliable Bum. "What's the field, anyway?"

"They's Fastworker. He ain't bad."

"What's Berny gonta enter?"

"That Gilt Girl invalid that hadda be lifted to one side to let our young Hopeless pass to-day. I guess both us and Berny'll be bidding nullos on the Commercial if we got good sense."

On Friday, the last day he was to run before the Commercial on Wednesday, the Bum was entered for the mile, which was too long for him, so no one took any interest until he stepped down the stretch an honorable third to the Whitney stables.

His family's hopes did an immediate Lazarus and Mae clattered down to the Bernheimer box not to miss one drop of the elixir of victory. But when Herb and Roy returned from the judges' stand she was back in her seat plainly dispirited.

"Bee acks like she's been takin' dope," she declared. "She never give me so much as a single dig. She's got circles under her eyes like feed bags. And Berny looks awful too."

"Roy," said Herb, "I got it. I been thinking a long

while Berny was bearing his barnful of crosses awful brave, but now I got it. I betcha he's up to tricks. I bet before dawn these mornings he's tryin' out that Gilt Girl filly. Just as Mae was talking I begun thinking about them leather pants they put on her every time she runs. They might as good send her out in a plaster cast. Accept it from Herbert, Berny's got his eye out for the Commercial."

The idea made Mae's heart stumble.

"Say!" said Roy.

"Think it over. You ain't see them try out the Gilt Girl at six o'clock when we was to the track, have you? What else have they got in their stables to ack so chipper about? Nothing but death and disease. Say, the odds on that filly'll be a million to one."

"Why, ain't they terrible?" Mae exclaimed. "Why, that ain't fair. Is that fair, Roy?"

But they were fighting as to which one should conceal himself under the hydrangeas in the yard of the house the Bernheimers were occupying and keep watch over their activities that night.

Mae, who always came to her husband's rescue on such occasions, pointed out that Roy wouldn't be any good as a sleuth. He'd just fall asleep and snore. He snored terrible. Besides, it wouldn't be proper for her to be left in the house alone with Herb. Finally Herb consented to undertake the vigil.

It was half past three when his shrill whistle from the stairs woke Mae.

"Get up, Roy," she said, and was out of bed, had a satin boudoir cap pulled over her hair and a green raincoat over her pajamas, while Roy was still rubbing his eyes and repeating, "Whassamatter, Mae?" in a voice of anguish.

"It's Herb. Get up."

"WazHerbwant?"

"Berny. We gotta follow Berny. C'mon. You always talk about me being slow."

Roy began fumbling into a dressing gown and Mae joined Herb.

"They's no call for you to come," he greeted her.

"I'd like to see me miss a trick like this. Didja have a terrible time?"

"Oh, no," Herb assured her. "No, it was swell. It didn't rain only three times, and there wasn't more than fifty or eighty mosquitoes in the bush I picked. Some was wired, but most of 'em was too mean to even carry a light. Where's Roy?"

"Luh, Roy!" Mae commanded, stamping her bare foot.

"I'm trying to find my bridgework," a sleepy voice answered.

"Aw, leave it out!" Herb cried. "C'mon. They got a awful head start."

Roy emerged sullenly.

"I bet Bee must run just like a grayhound," he said.

On the porch Mae remembered about having nothing on her feet and squealed for the men to wait for her while she ran to the hall closet where she grabbed two galoshes she thought belonged to the lady from whom they rented. Herb and Roy had started ahead, so she slipped them on and shuffled after. The street was black between arc lights.

One of the galoshes was no lady's. Mae didn't even know men's feet came in that size. She made a flapping sound when she hurried.

"What's the noise for?" Herb asked.

"I make it when I run," said Mae.

"It's a pity you wouldn't put on a bell."

"I can go slow quiet," Mae answered in a hoarse whisper. "Say, whatcha got on your feet, Roy?"

"Shoes."

"Say, gimme one. You could keep on this rub—"
Herb's hand over her mouth stopped her.

Ahead in the night a prosperous groan indicated where Bee Bernheimer plodded.

"What's the matter, Bee?" Berny's voice inquired.

"When we took up racing I thought it was carried on daytimes and you sat down to it."

"I guess you can't get ahead in nothing if you ain't willing to put yourself out."

"I ain't kicking, am I? Only it kinda winds me to walk. I gotta lotta pressure on my lungs, Berny. A woman built like me oughta be let have her sleep."

Mae didn't hear any more because Herb had forgotten that his hand was over her mouth and while she walked right on she was being smothered to death.

She bit Herb's hand as gently as she could and he swallowed an ouch and put it in his mouth.

"C'mon," Roy urged.

The minute Mae tried to quicken her pace the rubber flopped again.

"You go back," Herb told her.

"I will not."

"Keep quiet then. We could just as good have come in a autobus as have you along."

"Is that so?"

Mae was kept from more withering sarcasm by losing the big rubber and having to stop and fumble for it while Herb and Roy slipped away from her.

It was quite a time before she found it mouth down in a puddle.

She didn't even wait to let all the water run out because she hated being alone in the pitch dark with nothing on but black georgette pajamas under a raincoat and the town full of thugs.

"Hey, Roy!" she whispered as loudly as she dared, stumbling on blindly. "Hey, Herb! Hey, Roy!"

She'd gone quite a distance before a man jumped out from behind a tree and began choking her and saying, "Didn't I tell you to shut up?" which was reassuring because it was Herb.

"Where they gone?" Mae breathed.

"Trial track," Herb indicated its faintly visible white palings.

"C'mon," Roy urged again, and Herb threw himself down and wriggled under the fence. So did Roy, and Mae tried to, only she ran her head into a poplar tree and stunned herself so that she would have walked right into Berny and Bee where they stood talking with their trainer and a jockey if Roy hadn't seen her staggering past and tripped her up with his foot.

Mae was pretty mad by then, but all Herb and Roy were thinking about was what was being said in the other group.

Holley, the Bernheimers' trainer, was talking.

"We got a chance to see what time the baby makes on a wet track to-day," were his words, and as he spoke them he slapped the Gilt Girl affectionately. "I don't believe there's no mud that can stop her, tho. Joe'll let her out when he sees me light a match to get the time."

The jockey mounted and the Gilt Girl was led to the track. She could be heard making restive sounds.

Mr. Holley's match flared, and she was off. The single clicking volley of hoofbeats sounded incredibly speedy.

Herb kept his eyes glued to the luminous second hand of his watch. Roy counted it under his breath stuttering the numbers with excitement.

The Gilt Girl was back.

"Less'n one-eleven and a fi't'!" Holley stated.

"Hot Goophie!" Roy breathed.

Herb said, "I got it one-eleven flat."

"And we thought the Bum was flying when he did it in one-eleven-three."

"What we gonta do?" Mae demanded in a clamorous whisper. "I think we oughta expose 'em. Let's just walk right up and show we heard."

"Shush!" Both men went at her, and Roy added, "Expose 'em! Say, brains you got nix!"

"Well then, let's go back," Mae said. "I lost one of my galoshes by that tree where I hit my head."

"Will you shut up?" Herb asked.

"I think you're awful, Herb," Mae announced.

"G'wan and look for your old gumshoe if you wanta," Roy told her. "But shut up. We gotta stay here."

Mae waited in silence, standing on one foot like a resentful stork and holding to the thought that wet feet always gave her a cold on the chest.

The Gilt Girl ran twice more. Both times the trainer's stop watch confirmed Herb's one-eleven.

The Bernheimers were exultant.

"Good night, Mr. Holley," Bee minced. "I guess maybe you're gonta be worth what Mr. Bernheimer pays you, after all."

"Keep on working tho," Berny cautioned. "Now would be a bad time to get careless."

"Well, whadda you know?" Herb let out, as soon as they were beyond earshot.

"The Rawz!" Roy said. "The ripe red Rawz!"

Mae, however, usurped the opportunity to speak her mind.

"I think you fellas have treated me just awful," she proclaimed. "I'da felt bad if one of you hada come out on sumpin I wanted to do and lost his shoe and found it in water, and cracked his head, and lost it again. And I wouldn'ta tripped him up and just said 'shush' and 'shut up' to everything—"

Neither of them heard her.

"What you yelling razberry for?" Herb demanded of Roy. "Dontcha see that this is the hottest piece o' luck we coulda got? That filly ain't even been sighted by the dope hounds. We can get better odds on her than we coulda got on the Bum."

"Us get better odds? Us play Berny Bernheimer's horse?"

"This Gilt Girl's a sure thing. What's she gotta pass? Fastworker! Why, the Bum had Fastworker tied to the ribbon, and the Bum don't know one-eleven is on the clock."

Mae was listening to them by then.

"You mean you're gonna scratch the Bum?" she cried.

"What we gonna scratch him for?" Herb asked. "No point in lowering the odds that I can see, and if we was to scratch him Berny'd know we was hep. No, the Bum'll run all right, only you won't call it running when you see him crawl after that filly."

"You make me sick," Mae told him. "What you'd oughta do is tell everybody about Berny and Bee.

Why, they ain't no better than a coupla old crooks. I ain't afraid they'll win the Commercial. I don't believe that filly is half as good as the Bum."

"Can you beat it?" Roy demanded, almost in tears from exasperation. "Didncha hear what they clocked it?"

"What can you tell about the way a horse runs in the dark, anyhow?" Mae insisted. "It ain't gonna be dark when she runs the Commercial, is it?"

"I suppose all the sports that try out their ponies at night, and always has tried them out at night, is fools? Well, they ain't. Everybody knows a horse runs better when it can see."

"Well, don't bite me," Mae protested. "I was just saying what I got a right to think. I betcha on my Bum."

"All right, you bet me and that's where your betting stops," Roy said. "I hope you get a lotta fun off it."

"Do you mean I can't put nothing on my pony in the Commercial? Not even a ten-spot for sentiment?"

The hour had completely destroyed Roy's disposition.

"You guessed just right for once," he said.

That morning after dawn the Bum did what anyone who knew his congenital contrariness might have expected of him. He ran his tryout six furlongs in one-eleven and two-fifths. It made Roy uneasy about Herb's plan.

"He's gettin' awful good, Herb," he protested shakily.

Herb's was a stubborn nature. Roy's weak-mindedness changed his idea into an obsession.

"You're a punk looker, then," he roared. "I told you the Bum wouldn't win, and that's enough."

"But look at the first day," Roy said. "Mock couldn't hold him in."

"It ain't gonta be Mock this time does the holding," Herb answered. "I done a little shopping yesterday, and I wasn't gonta tell you, so if anything come up you'd be out of it, but now you asked for it, and here goes. I bought a little chloral hydrate. You know what that is? Well, when shot into the Bum it'll give him the stoopidest streak he's had yet, and when I say that I've said a idiot. Now I've got it and I know how to use it, and I know it'll work. Will that shut your mouth or won't it? Because if it won't we quit, see?"

It would.

Indeed, at dinner when Mae began tentatively, "You changed your mind about that ten-spot, ain't you, Roy?" he replied courteously, "Yes, I have like the Fairy Queen," and Herb prayed, "Oh, Momma, just gimme patience till I reach my razor!"

Mae resolved to keep her mouth shut from then on, but it wasn't until she went to bed that she realized how good and mad she was. It was a novel sensation.

She sat up and ran out her tongue at Le Roy, who lay beside her in uproarious unconsciousness.

"I guess I earn my money, Meanie!" she said.

She was as cold and proud at breakfast as she had it in her to be, and when Herb said, "Dream about corn on the cob again, Gipsy Queen?" merely replied, "Well, I did, if you wanta know."

Roy resented discipline.

"I guess we better eat lunch up to the track, Herb," he said, meaning away from Mae, who hated to be left alone for meals.

She tried to make her "Y'can if y'wanta" sound indifferent.

When they found her in the clubhouse, however, Mae had gotten over her mad. Few people, and certainly not Mae, could have resisted the afternoon. There were ninety-three million miles of sheer sunlight over the track. The fountains were throwing great spoutfuls of crystal beads. The deep green of the grass, the bright, clear colors of jockey blouses and sporty motor cars, the excitement of a bumper crowd, and a band moaning a Mammy song with besotted emotion-alism, were the heady ingredients for a perfect cocktail of an occasion.

Altho Herb and Roy had kept her waiting until after the first race before they appeared to take her to the Bum's stall, which they always did before Mae's pet was to run, she greeted them with an almost guilty cordiality.

Their tardiness had been intentional. Herb had paid his professional visit to the Bum earlier in the day and was wary of inspection. The Commercial was the third race, and they'd planned that if they took Mae just before the second they could hurry her away on the pretext of not missing that event, before she noticed too much.

Mockton was dressing, so Waltie, the moron, was on guard at the Bum's stall. Seeing them in the distance, he scuttled away as usual.

Waltie's noisy departure should have left Reliable Bum trembling and jumpy. Instead he stood stock still, head down.

Mae gave one glance at him.

"My pony's sick," she cried. "Look at him, Herb. He looks terrible. Y'oughta had him scratched. He hadn't oughta run."

"Got one a his stoopid streaks," Herb growled.

"That's all the sick he is. We gotta get back if we don't wanta miss the second."

"Whadda I care about the second?" Mae asked, pushing into the Bum's stall. "I tell you he's sick. Him's sicky boy."

The Bum turned lackluster eye and hot nose away from her.

"We gotta send for a vet," she announced. "You go for a vet, right this minute, Roy."

Her words struck terror to both of them. If Mae was so convinced at one glance, what would the rest of the world say? Roy tried to argue with her.

"Say, will you listen to reason, Mae? I've seen the Bum like this lotsa times. We got our fish on Gilt Girl at forty to one. They's no use getting upset if the Bum is gonta lose."

"I ain't worrying about losing or not losing," Mae answered. "I'm worried about my pony. I ain't gonta leave him and not do sumpin. We gotta have a vet. You heard what I said, Roy. Go on now."

It was a very real crisis. There was ringing authority in Mae's tones, and Roy actually looked as tho he meant to obey her.

Herb Twitchell knew it was up to him to do something.

"Where's he going to get a vet, Mae?" he stalled.

"There's one on the street we come through to the track. I've seen his sign every day," Mae said. "Go get him, Roy."

"Wait a minute," Herb held up her imperiousness. "Maybe there's one at the track Roy or me could find. But while we're looking why don't you run down to this place you're talking about and see if you can get that one? Not that the Bum needs it—"

"I should say I will," Mae returned. "You don't haveta ask me twice." And she made off.

"Say, are you crazy?" her husband demanded of his partner. "Why, these vets are all in with the big guys. Why, just let one get a squint at the Bum and we never would get let on the track again."

"Shut up," Herb answered. "I was just getting rida her. You don't think any vet in this town sits home while races are being run out here, do you? What you got on your hip?"

"I ain't got nothing, Herb. Them highballs took the last drop. You don't wanta drink now, anyhow, Herb. You gotta keep your head and do sumpin. If Mae was wise, dontcha think they'd get wise in the judges' stand? You'd oughta do sumpin, Herb."

"That's what I want the hooch for, boob. If we can slip the Bum a good shotta whisky, he'll wake up so nobody'd have an idea—"

Herb broke off to shout "Waltie" at the top of his lungs.

While he was waiting for a response he turned on Le Roy furiously.

"Whatcha waiting for me for, Mushhead?" he demanded furiously. "Dash the body around and see if you can't raise some licker yourself."

Le Roy scooted off, the very slant of his neck proclaiming agitation.

*"Waltie!"*

For all his masterfulness, Herb was quivering inwardly. If the Bum were generally recognized as a doped horse, there would be hot reckonings to pay, and time was pressing. The second race was being run.

Waltie's scared monkey face peered around one corner of the stable.

"You hearse horse," Herb addressed him. "What
you so slow about? I gotta beat it, and I want you to
get this straight before I go. No one is to get let to
look at the Bum while I'm gone. Get me?"

"Yas, Mistawh Twitchell," Waltie wabbled out.

"You better," Herb menaced, then he was off in the
direction diametrically opposite that Roy had taken.


His quest would have seemed an easy one to any but
a pessimist, but an arrant pessimist Herb was, and this
time he was right. Raising a flask from any of his
friends that afternoon was just about as easy as the
job of a firing squad. He tried a dozen friends until
at last an entire stranger, who'd heard one of the con-
ferences, came to the rescue.

"Here's some gin, buddy," he said, producing a large
bottle. "It's homemade, but it's O. K."

That would probably do.

"Much obliged," Herb said, and snatching the bottle
started back.

The stranger, who'd expected him to take a drink and
return the rest, looked a little as tho someone had
pulled out the chair in which he was about to sit.

"Lady fainting," Herb improvised over his shoulder.

He'd gotten what seemed like a mile away from the
Bum's stable. Just before he reached it he ran into
Roy, who was panting and distraught.

"All right," Herb gasped.

Roy waggled his head in token of understanding or
something.

"Go on, head off that gas meter you married," Herb
managed further. "She might find somebody."

Roy panted some more and nodded again, and as Herb dashed on he saw Roy make for the direction Mae had taken.

At the stable Herb took out the cork and ran to the Bum's stall.

"Look here," he said to Waltie. "You can be just as half-witted as you wanta be all the resta your life, but you gotta do this for me now. You gotta hold the Bum while I pour this down his throat."

Waltie's face looked like one of those rubber ones you squeeze.

"He kicks awful," he moaned. "Seems like he'd bite."

"If he bites your arm off you gotta do it," Herb told him. "D'you hear me? D'you hear me?"

There must have been some old Legree blood in Herb. A blubbering assent came from Waltie.

The Bum put up a surprizingly game fight for his non-alcoholic principles, and Waltie was swung about in the air for some minutes like the girl who stopped the curfew, but at last Herb got a good swig down the animal.

Herb and Waltie both half fell out of the stall, and Mockton, coming in search of his mount, wore to the eyes of both the radiance of an archangel.

The Gilt Girl paraded at the head of the line and caused a little ripple of surprise. She was arch and fine. Her tiny hoofs seemed hardly to touch the ground. She sparkled like champagne.

Fastworker, a conventionally magnificent beast, claimed a hand from stand and clubhouse.

Roy had met Mae, who was hurrying back to the track, alone and angry, assured her that they'd found a

S. S. X-7

vet who said the Bum was all right, and brought her
to their usual seats.

Mae had been feeling better until she saw Fastworker, when it struck her, for the first time, that he
was going to win. Almost everyone else had known it
all along.

"Fastworker don't look so bad," she gulped.

"Bad hocks," Roy asseverated.

Herb staggered up, the picture of exhaustion, but
Mae was seeing Reliable Bum and had no eyes for him.

"My pony's feeling better," she squealed. "You just
watch my pony."

The Bum was, indeed, not unlike himself on former
occasions except that what had been contemptuous
indifference before now seemed seasoned with a certain
roguish braggadocio. He reared three times before the
stand. The whites of his eyes were very noticeable.

Roy cupped his hand to Herb's ear.

"That musta been good stuff."

"Yeah," Herb answered. "I wasn't sure gin would
do it."

"Gin! That was genuine old Bourbon."

Herb gaped.

"That I give him?"

"No, that I did. Did you—? Didn't Waltie tell
you?"

The wild surmise in each pair of eyes became a
certainty.

"My Gawd!" Herb muttered. "I bet he'll bust."

They couldn't have talked so long without queries
from Mae except that she was absorbed in her glasses,
which were trained on Reliable Bum.

As usual, the Bum was holding up the start. His

giddy leaps in the air, and unreasoned boltings seemed to affect all the line-up.

"Looks like he was posting a non-union shop," Mae said nervously.

Mockton was more afraid of his mount than usual. All his effort was confined to sticking on. Finally the sight of his ineffectuality led the starter to shout:

"Pull up that dawg, and give him the whip."

In his agitation Mockton welcomed the voice of authority. He pulled till his scrawny arms ached, and struck violently.

The whip had always plunged the Bum into his most profound stupidities. Just at that moment, however, when he was wavering between the effects of the opiate and the stimulation of the burning liquors within him, the whip was a dangerous experiment. It might have turned the Bum into a killer or a heap of carcass. It happened to turn him into a race horse.

The line joggled straight, the cord flew up. There was thunder and dust and a cry from the stand.

Mae's glasses discerned Sam's cerise in the mêlée, and she opened her mouth.

Bee, who never could focus her glasses, tugged at Berny.

"Is it her, Berny?"

Berny's eyes were dim with the sweat of anguish. He shook off his wife.

"I ain't got it yet. Don't pull, Bee."

The horses swept around the curve. The one ahead wasn't the Gilt Girl or Reliable Bum. Fastworker was ahead running a race.

"Reliable Bum," Mae yelled, as she had the first day. "Oh, you Reliable Bum!"

It was Reliable Bum second by a length.

"Win for yer Momma!" Mae yelled.

Tremendous and inspiring as was her cry, it is doubt-
ful whether the Bum heard. The Bum was too busy
for encouragement. He was horizontal with effort,
pushing great combustible strides.

"Fastworker!" the stand petitioned. "Fastworker!"
the clubhouse implored.

Mae's cry shamed the multiple effort.

"Reliable Bum! *Reliable Bum!* OH, YOU RELIABLE
BUM!"

And the Bum gained. In that incredibly long endur-
ing passage of the stand he crept up steadily. At the
corner of the clubhouse he passed Fastworker. He kept
ahead, crossed the line, ran on and on, unstoppable,
jubilant, drunken.

"Crikes!" Herb said simply.

Roy keened, "Hot Goophie!" like a whole Irish
peasantry in a peat bog.

"Wha' did I tell you?" Mae yelled. "Who laughed
at me because I dreamed about corn on the cob."

"Lotta luck it brought," Herb groaned. "Us without
a cent up on the Bum."

"Yeah, I would crow, if I was you," Roy pitched in.
"If that's your idea of luck, you like being broke
better than me. The odds on him was twenty to one
and us counting on that night-blooming filly."

They couldn't deflate Mae.

"Didn't I tell ya," she caroled, "that a horse they
had to sneak out at night to run wasn't gonta be good
for nothing in a race?"

All three had forgotten how near they were to the
Bernheimer box. The Bernheimers, sunk in the gloom
of defeated hopes, had at least had the solace of believ-

ing those hopes to have been secret. The words were salt in their wounds.

Herb and Roy got to their feet to start for the judges' stand, but suddenly they found themselves confronted by an irate Berny shaking his bediamonded fist.

"Listen here, you, before you go down. I got a good mind to go down and tell what I suspect, you dirty crooks. How did it happen you hadn't a cent up on your horse, huh? You had fixed up some dirty work for that horse not to win."

"Yeah. Yeah. I bet it's true," Bee was saying in the background.

Usually Herb would have been more than equal to such an occasion, but he was almost worn out and so was Roy. They stood stupidly.

It was Mae who flashed forth.

"Say, are you crazy?" she demanded. "Just because a horse wins, do you think that's any reason for going down and claiming that he was doped to lose?"

"But they didn't have no money up on him," Berny cried.

"They didn't," Mae answered. "Because, as Bee *very kindly* pointed out, they ain't been very flush lately. But I did. I had five hundred fish up at twenty to one —every centa back alimony Vernon owed. Does that sound very much like they was any dirt going on? Does it, I ast you?"

After the ceremonies the boys were pretty abject to Mae.

"Say, you were swell what you said to Berny," they told her. "Was it true what you said about the five hundred?"

"Sure, it was!" Mae answered. "Oh, it's awful about

Vernon, tho.   My lawyers got it off him just before
he was sent up the river for a stretch.   Poor Vernon,
he's gonta hate the pen.   He's an awful elegant kinda
fella.   I'm gonta send some back to him.   I guess
maybe I'll send the whole five hundred or more."

"Aw, Mae!   When me and Herb is broke?"

"Well, you both been treating me pretty mean lately,"
Mae said.   "And I'm gonna blow myself to a sweet
pretty little dress I've had my eye on and a lotta other
things and—"

"And we don't get none?" Roy questioned.

Herb plucked at his sleeve.

"Dontcha plague her now," he advised.   "We'll get
ours, all right.   You know Mae."

# I'M IN A HURRY

## By William Hazlett Upson

Dry River Junction, Texas.
October 1, 1924.

To The Farmers Friend Tractor Company,
Earthworm City, Illinois.

Dear Sir: I'm in a hurry I want a new main drive gear for my tractor. This tractor was formerly owned by Joe Banks of Llano, Texas, and bought by me at the auction after he died. The main drive gear in the tractor has busted and I just been over and asked the widow Banks where Joe used to buy parts for his tractors and she said she aint sure but she thinks it was The Farmers Friend Tractor Company, Earthworm City, Illinois. So please let me know if you are the folks, and if so please send the gear at once. As I am in a hurry. It is the main drive gear. It is the big bull gear in the back end of the transmission that goes round and round and drives the tractor excuse this paper as my regular business letter paper has not come yet yours truly,

DAVID CROCKETT SUGGS.

---

FARMERS' FRIEND TRACTOR COMPANY
MAKERS OF EARTHWORM TRACTORS

Earthworm City, Ill.
October 3, 1924.

Mr. David Crockett Suggs,
Dry River Junction, Tex.

Dear Sir: This will acknowledge receipt of your letter of October 1, in which we note that you request us to send you a gear for your tractor.

(Copyright, 1925, by William Hazlett Upson.)

In this connection we are pleased to advise that an inspection of our files reveals the fact that Mr. Joseph Banks of Llano, Tex., was the owner of one of our old-style Model 45 Earthworm Tractors. Mr. Banks acquired this tractor on June 3, 1915. We are changing our records to indicate that this tractor has been purchased by yourself, and we are most happy to assure you that all the resources of the Farmers' Friend Tractor Company are at your service and that we can supply you promptly with everything you may need in the way of spare parts, service and information.

We regret, however, that your description of the gear which you desire is not sufficient for us to identify same, as there are a number of gears in the transmission to which the description "main drive gear" might conceivably apply. Kindly look up this gear in the parts book and advise us the proper part number and name as given therein. When necessary information is received, immediate shipment will be made.

In the meantime, we wish to extend you a most cordial welcome into the happy family of Earthworm users, to congratulate you upon selecting an Earthworm Tractor—even tho it be of such an old model—and to assure you of our constant interest and desire to cooperate with you to the fullest extent.

Very truly yours,<br>
FREDERICK R. OVERTON,<br>
Parts Department.

———

Dry River Junction, Texas.<br>
October 6, 1924.

To The Farmers Friend Tractor Company,
Earthworm City, Illinois.

Dear Sir: I got your letter I got no parts book. I asked the widow of Joe Banks, who is the man that owned the tractor before I bought it at the auction after he died, I asked her did they have a parts book for the tractor and she said they once had a parts book but it is lost. I would look up the gear in the parts book if I could, but you can understand that I can't look up the gear in the parts book if I got no parts book. What I want is the big bull gear way at the back. The great big cog wheel with 44 cogs on it that goes round and round and drives the tractor.

I'm in a hurry because the tractor is unfortunately broke down right while I'm doing a very important job for Mr. Rogers of this city. The tractor run fine until 3 p. m. October 1, when there came a loud and very funny noise in the back and the tractor would no longer pull. We took the cover off the transmission case, and this big cog wheel was busted. Six cogs was busted off of it, and the tractor will not pull, only make a funny noise.

I am a young man 24 years of age just starting in business and expect to get married soon, so please send the gear at once as I'm in a hurry and oblige,

DAVID CROCKETT SUGGS.

---

FARMERS' FRIEND TRACTOR COMPANY
MAKERS OF EARTHWORM TRACTORS

Earthworm City, Ill.
October 9, 1924.

Mr. David Crockett Suggs,
Dry River Junction, Tex.

Dear Sir: This will acknowledge your valued letter of October 6, stating that you desire a gear for your tractor, but are unable to give us the parts number of same owing to the fact that you have no parts book. We have carefully gone over your description of the gear, but we regret that we have been unable positively to identify what gear it is that you desire. We note that you state the gear has 44 teeth and we feel sure that some mistake has been made, as there is no 44-tooth gear in the tractor.

We are therefore mailing you under separate cover a parts book for the Model 45 Earthworm Tractor, Year 1915, and would suggest that you look up the gear in this book, and let us know the part number so that we can fill your order.

Unfortunately we are not able to supply you a parts book printed in English.

Nearly all of the old-style Model 45 tractors were sold to the French Government in 1915 to be used in pulling artillery on the western front. As only a few of these tractors were sold in America, the edition of English parts books was very limited and has been exhausted. We are, however, sending you one of the French parts books.

We regret exceedingly that we are obliged to give you a parts book printed in a foreign language; and we realize, of course, that possibly you may be unable to understand it. However, you should be able to find the desired gear in the pictures, which are very plain.

Kindly give us the part number which is given under the picture of the gear, and we will make immediate shipment.

Very truly yours,
FREDERICK R. OVERTON,
Parts Department.

Dry River Junction, Texas.
October 12, 1924.

To The Farmers Friend Tractor Company,
Earthworm City, Illinois.

Dear Sir: Your letter has come your book has come
you was right when you said I might not understand
it. I cant understand the Dago printing and I been
looking at the pictures all evening and I cant understand the pictures they dont look like nothing I ever
seen. So I can't give you no part number, but I'm
in a hurry so please send the gear anyway. It is
the one way at the back. You cant miss it. Its not
the one that lays down its the one that sets up on edge
and has 44 teeth and meshes with the little one with
12 teeth. The little one goes round and round and
drives the big one. And the big one is keyed on the
main shaft and goes round and round and drives the
tractor. Or I should say used to go round and round,
but now it has six teeth busted out and wont go
round—only makes a funny noise when it gets to the
place where the teeth are busted out.

I'm in a hurry and to show you that I need this gear
quick, I will explain that the tractor is laid up right in
the middle of an important job I'm doing for Mr.
Rogers of this city. I'm a young man, age 24 years,
and new at the house moving business and I want
to make a good impression and also expect to get
married soon.

When Mr. Rogers of this city decided to move his
house from down by the depot up to the north end
of town, and give me the job, I thought it was a fine
chance to get started in business and make a good
impression. I got the house jacked up, and I put
heavy timbers underneath, and trucks with solid wheels

that I bought from a contractor at Llano. And I bought this second-hand tractor from Joe Banks at Llano at the auction after he died, and all my money is tied up in this equipment and on October 1, at 3 p. m. we had the house moved half way to where they want it, when the tractor made a funny noise and quit. And if I don't get new gear pretty soon and move the house the rest of the way I'll be a blowed up sucker.

I'm just starting in business and want to make a good impression and I'm expecting to get married so please hurry with the gear. Excuse paper as my regular business paper has not come yet and oblige,

DAVID CROCKETT SUGGS.

---

FARMERS' FRIEND TRACTOR COMPANY
MAKERS OF EARTHWORM TRACTORS

Earthworm City, Ill.
October 14, 1924.

Mr. David Crockett Suggs,
Dry River Junction, Tex.

Dear Sir: This will acknowledge your valued favor of October 12, and we regret exceedingly that you have been unable to locate the part which you desire in the parts book, and that consequently you have been subject to annoying delay. As it is always our desire to render the greatest possible service to Earthworm Tractor owners, we have gone into this matter with the greatest of care; and after checking over very thoroughly the descriptions given in your latest letter and also in former letters, we have come to the conclusion that the gear you desire is the 45-tooth intermediate spur gear, symbol number 6843, as illustrated on page 16 of the parts book. We note that you state the gear has 44 teeth, but as there is no such gear in your model tractor, and as No. 6843 gear fits the description in other particulars, we can only assume that you made a mistake in counting the number of teeth in the gear.

Accordingly we are shipping you by express this afternoon one No. 6843 gear, which we trust will prove to be the part desired. Assuring you of our constant desire to render you every possible service, efficiently and promptly, I remain,

Very truly yours,

FREDERICK R. OVERTON,

Parts Department.

---

Dry River Junction, Texas,
October 18, 1924.

To The Farmers Friend Tractor Company,
Earthworm City, Illinois.

Dear Sir: Your letter come yesterday your gear come to-day C. O. D. $41.26 and not only that, but it is no good and it wont fit. It is not like the old gear. It looks like a well made gear but there is nothing like it on my tractor so it is no good to me it is too big it won't go on it won't fit on the shaft. And if it did fit on the shaft, it would not work because it is too big and the teeth would not mesh with the teeth on the little gear, and it ought to have 44 teeth like I said, *not* 45.

So will you look this up again more carefully and send me the right gear and send it as quick as possible? I'm in a hurry, and I will explain to you how things stand so you can see I am no liar when I say I got to have this gear right off or I am a blowed up sucker.

I am new in the house moving business and I am moving a house for Mr. Rogers of this city, and Mr. Rogers is a very stubborn old cuss and he insisted that the house be moved all together—which includes the main part which is two stories high and built very strong and solid, and also the front porch which sticks out in front and is built pretty weak, and also the one-story kitchen which sticks out behind. The kitchen is very frail.

But Mr. Rogers did not listen to me when I wanted to move the kitchen and front porch separate from the house. So, as I am a young man and new at the house moving business and anxious to make a good impression, I tried to do it like he wanted. I jacked up the whole works all together, and put timbers underneath, and heavy trucks that I bought from a contractor at Llano, and we came up from the depot fine—the tractor pulling good and the little old house rolling along smooth and quiet and beautiful. But at 3 p. m. October 1, just as we was going past Jim Ferguson's Drug Store on the main street of this city, there come a funny noise in the tractor, and we have been stuck ever since waiting for a new gear because the tractor will not run with six teeth busted out of the old gear.

So you can see that it is no lie that I am in a hurry, and I will explain that for 2 and ½ weeks, no traffic has been able to go past Jim Ferguson's Drug Store. All traffic on the main street of this city has been detoured—turning to the right through the field next to Johnson's Garage, following the back lane past the shed where Harvey Jenkins keeps his cow, and then around Wilson's Hardware Store and back to the main street, and all this owing to the stubbornness of old man Rogers making me take the porch and the kitchen along at the same time.

The porch is now resting two feet from the drug store and the kitchen just three feet from the post office on the other side of the street. If old man Rogers had listened to me and we had taken the kitchen off, there would have been room for traffic to get past, but now we can't take the kitchen off on account of being so jammed up against the post office, but people don't figger on that and everybody in town blames it on me that traffic is held up, which is very wrong as I am doing the best I can.

And now old man Rogers says I contracted to move his house, and I had better hurry up, and he says why don't I hire some horses but I say horses would be unsafe, because when they get to pulling something very heavy they get to jerking and they would be liable to jerk the house and injure it, owing to the fact that Mr. Rogers was so stubborn as to make me leave the kitchen and the porch on the house, thus weakening it. And besides I got no money to waste hiring horses when I got a tractor already, so you can see why I'm in a hurry being anxious to make a good impression and get married.

Please send at once the right gear which has FORTY-FOUR TEETH (44), because the old gear has 38 good teeth, and 6 busted off, making 44 like I said, *not* 45. And the right gear is an inch narrower than the one you sent, and the hole through the middle is smaller. I am making a picture so you can see just what gear it is, so please send it at once and oblige.

DAVID CROCKETT SUGGS.

FARMERS' FRIEND TRACTOR COMPANY
MAKERS OF EARTHWORM TRACTORS

Earthworm City, Ill.
October 21, 1924.

Mr. David Crockett Suggs,
Dry River Junction, Tex.

Dear Sir: This will acknowledge receipt of your letter
of October 18, from which we note that you are having
trouble in installing in your tractor gear No. 6843,
which we shipped you on October 14.

We regret exceedingly that you have had this trouble,
and to the end that the basis of the difficulty might be
discovered, we have carefully checked over your former
correspondence and have at length come to the conclusion that gear No. 6843, which we sent you, is the
proper gear. We are therefore at a loss to understand
why you have been unable to use it, and can only suggest that you may possibly have made some error in
installing it.

To obviate this difficulty we are to-day mailing you,
under separate cover, a copy of our latest instruction
book on the care, operation and repair of Earthworm
Tractors. We regret that this book was prepared for
the new-style tractors, but as the method of installing
transmission gears is essentially the same in both old
and new style tractors, we feel sure that you will have
no trouble in applying the instructions to your old-style
tractor. Please study carefully the pictures and full
descriptions on page 34, and if you proceed as directed
we feel sure you will experience no further difficulty in
installing the gear.

In case, however, there still remains some minor
trouble to interfere with the perfect operation of the
tractor, we shall appreciate it if you will notify us, as

we are always anxious to give owners of Earthworm Tractors the fullest possible cooperation.

Very truly yours,<br>FREDERICK R. OVERTON,<br>Parts Department.

———

Dry River Junction, Texas.<br>October 25, 1924.

To The Farmers Friend Tractor Company,
Earthworm City, Illinois.

Dear Sir: Your letter come yesterday your book come to-day they are no good to me. It takes more than a book for a new tractor to put onto an entirely different old tractor a gear wheel that don't belong to it. I tell you again—you have sent me the wrong gear.

What I want is the big bull gear on the back that has 44 teeth. FORTY-FOUR. *Not* 45. And it goes round and round and makes the tractor go. It is the great big cog wheel that meshes with the little cog wheel. I bet you have sent me a gear for one of your new-style tractors—how do I know? You told me you had looked it up what model tractor I got, so why don't you send me the gear that will fit?

If you people knew what I was up against, you would get busy, and you would send me that gear in a hurry. The whole town is sore at me. And I will explain that this is a big place with trolley cars and everything.

The trolleys here run on a track, but they are not electric, they are run by gasoline motors inside, and are very modern and up-to-date like everything else in this city. And for over three weeks now the trolley from the depot has been coming up almost as far as Jim Ferguson's Drug Store, and then it has to stop and the conductor will give the people transfers. And they will get out and squeeze past old man Rogers's house, and get on the other trolley and ride on. And it is lucky they have two cars. A few years ago they only had one.

And old man Rogers says if I don't get action by the first of the week, he is going to hire horses himself, and pull the house where he wants it. And if I expect to get a cent for it I can just sue him, and he says he is tired of living in a house sitting in the middle of the street with the front porch poking into the drug store window and the people kidding him all the time. But it's all on account of his own foolishness and stubbornness, because I told him he had better go live with his brother in Llano while the house was being moved, but he is a guy that you can't tell him nothing and so he is living there with Mrs. Rogers and daughter Mildred, and Mrs. Rogers is cooking on an oil stove on account they don't know coal is safe in moving, and now they blame it on me because the oil stove smokes up the whole house. So you can see I'm in a hurry, and everybody is sore because the traffic is detoured, and me having to hang red lanterns on the house every night so people won't run into it, and the Police Department has served notice on me that I got until next Thursday to move the house or get pinched. And they had given me a permit to move the house. But they say a permit ain't no 99-year lease. And that just shows how it is—they all try to make mean cracks like that.

And this afternoon, old Mr. Rogers came up to me and he said, "Dave, I hope you ain't still thinking of getting married?"

And I said, "I sure am," because, as I told you in another letter, I'm expecting to get married.

Then Mr. Rogers said, "I may have something to say about that, young man." And I will explain that it is possible that old Mr. Rogers—whose house I am moving with my tractor—may have some influence in the matter, owing to the fact that the girl I expect to marry is named Mildred Rogers, and unfortunately happens to be the daughter of old Mr. Rogers.

So you see, I want that gear, and I want it quick. I am sending back the new gear please credit me with the $41.26 I paid on the C. O. D. I am also sending you the old busted gear. Please look over the old busted gear and send me one just like it, only with the six teeth not busted out. Please hurry and remember FORTY-FOUR TEETH, and oblige yours truly,

DAVID CROCKETT SUGGS.

P. S. *Not* 45 teeth.

———

FARMERS' FRIEND TRACTOR COMPANY<br>MAKERS OF EARTHWORM TRACTORS

Earthworm City, Ill.<br>October 29, 1924.

Mr. David Crockett Suggs,
Dry River Junction, Tex.

Dear Sir: This will acknowledge your valued favor of October 26 in reference to the trouble you are having with your tractor. We regret exceedingly that the misunderstanding in regard to the gear which you need has caused you the annoying delay which you mention.

As soon as your old gear arrives, it will be checked up and every possible effort will be made to supply you promptly with a duplicate of it.

Very truly yours,<br>FREDERICK R. OVERTON,<br>Parts Department.

DAVID CROCKETT SUGGS
CONTRACTOR
HOUSES MOVED SAFELY, SPEEDILY AND SURELY

Dry River Junction, Texas.
October 31, 1924.

To The Farmers Friend Tractor Company,
Earthworm City, Illinois.

Dear Sir: My new letter paper has come your letter has come please send me the gear as quick as possible. I'm in a hurry more than at any time before and unless I can get this mess straightened out I'll be more of a blowed up sucker than anybody you ever seen, and in order that you may see what a rush I am in and send the gear as quick as possible, I will explain 2 very unfortunate events which has took place since my last letter. The first was last night.

Being Thursday night and my regular night to call, I went around to see Miss Mildred Rogers, who, as I have explained before, I had expected to marry very soon, and who used to live down by the depot, but is now located temporarily on Main Street just in front of Ferguson's Drug Store. It is not as much fun as it used to be to call at the Rogers's house. Formerly it was possible to sit in the hammock on the front porch, and as the house set back from the street and there was trees around and no street lights, a very pleasant evening could be had.

But at present the front porch is located in a most unfortunate way just two feet from the windows of Ferguson's Drug Store, which is all lighted up—you know how drug store windows is—lots of big white lights, and all kinds of jars full of colored water with more lights shining through. And people squeezing past between the porch and the drug store and going in to get ice cream sodas or stopping to crack bum jokes about me, which I will not repeat. So you can see that it would not be any fun for me and Mildred to sit in the hammock in the evening, even if it was possible to sit in the hammock which it is not, owing to the fact that the porch pillar to which the hammock is fastened has become so weakened by the jacking up of the house that it would take very little to pull it over and let the whole porch roof down with a bang.

So we decided that we better sit in the parlor and we had no sooner entered and I was not doing any harm in any way when old Mr. Rogers came in and there was a very painful scene which I won't describe only to say that he used such expressions as "Get to Hell out of here," and "I don't want my daughter keeping company with any moron," which is a word he got out of the Dallas News.

So after he had hollered around and Mildred had cried, I left the house in a dignified manner. Being a gentleman and always respectful to old age, I did not talk back to him, the dirty crook. But you can see why it is I am in a hurry for the gear.

The other unfortunate event was just this a. m., when old man Rogers went out and hired twelve horses from all over town and also one small size flivver tractor to move his house up to where he wants it. He tried to get a big tractor, but there is none in town or nearby except mine which is broke down. But there is plenty of horses and there is this little flivver tractor that would not be big enough to pull the house all by itself.

So this morning they wheeled my poor old tractor out of the way, and they hooked up to the house and there was about a hundred people from the town and from round about that was helping with advice and hollering and yelling and telling Mr. Rogers how to do it. And there was I—the only practical and professional house-mover in the whole city—and none of them asked my advice about anything and so it is not my fault what happened.

When they was all ready, Mr. Rogers he stands up and hollers out, "All ready,—Go!" And the six drivers yelled at the twelve horses, and all the people standing around began to cheer and shout. And the feller on the little flivver tractor started up the motor so quick it made a big noise and scared the horses and all the horses began jumping and heaving and they jerked the house sidewise, and some of the timbers slipped, and the kitchen that I told you about,—it give a little lurch and fell off the house. Just let go, and fell off.

So that scared them, and they unhooked the horses and the flivver tractor and didn't try no more moving, and the house is still there all except the kitchen which was busted up so bad that they finished the job and knocked it to pieces and took it away in wheel barrows.

One good thing is that now the traffic can get in between the house and the Post Office so they don't have to detour any more. But one very unfortunate thing was that Mrs. Rogers happened to be in the kitchen when it fell off being shaken up considerable but not seriously injured so you can see that I got to have the tractor running again so I can move the house and I hope you will send the gear at once yours truly and oblige.

DAVID CROCKETT SUGGS.

FARMERS' FRIEND TRACTOR COMPANY
MAKERS OF EARTHWORM TRACTORS

Earthworm City, Ill.
November 2, 1924.

Mr. David Crockett Suggs,
Dry River Junction, Tex.

Dear Sir: This will acknowledge your valued favor of October 31 requesting that we use all possible haste in sending you a gear which you need to repair your tractor. We are also pleased to report the receipt of one No. 6843 gear which we shipped you on October 14 and which you returned unused owing to the fact that it will not fit your tractor. We are crediting your account with $41.26 C. O. D. which you paid on this shipment.

The broken gear which you sent as a sample has been carefully checked over by our Engineering Department. They report that they have been unable to identify this gear, and they are of the opinion that no gear similar to this has ever been manufactured by this company. We are, therefore, at a loss to under-stand how this gear ever came to be in your tractor. We do not make gears similar to the one you have sent in, and it will therefore be impossible for us to supply you with one. However, it is always our policy to be of the greatest possible service to Earthworm owners, and we would suggest that the best thing to do in the circumstances would be for one of our service mechanics to inspect your machine.

Fortunately, it happens that Dry River Junction is the nearest railroad point to the Canyon Ranch, which has just purchased a Ten-Ton Earthworm Tractor. Consequently, Mr. Luke Torkle, one of our service men, will be at Dry River Junction in a few days to unload this tractor and drive it overland to the ranch

If you desire, we will have Mr. Torkle stop off and inspect your machine, advising you what steps to take to put it into first-class running condition; or, if this is impossible, to confer with you in regard to turning in your old machine and purchasing one of our new models. Kindly let us know what you wish us to do in this matter.

Very truly yours,

FREDERICK R. OVERTON,
Parts Department.

———

### TELEGRAM

Dry River Junc Tex Nov 4 1924
Farmers Friend Tractor Co
Earthworm Cy, Ills

*Have the guy come quick in a hurry.*

DAVID CROCKETT SUGGS.

———

### FARMERS' FRIEND TRACTOR COMPANY
### SERVICE MAN'S REPORT

WRITTEN AT: Dry River Junction, Tex.
DATE: November 7, 1924.
WRITTEN BY: Luke Torkle, Serviceman.
SUBJECT: Tractor belonging to D. C. Suggs.

Reached here 7 a. m. Unloaded tractor for Canyon Ranch, and will drive it over to-morrow.

Before I had a chance to look up D. C. Suggs, the mayor and prominent citizens urgently requested me to use the new tractor to move a house that was blocking the main street. This looked like good advertizing for us, especially as the county commissioner here is expecting to buy a tractor for road work. Accordingly, I spent the morning moving the house to where they wanted it, and then looked up Mr. Suggs.

Found he has left town. It is reported that he was shot at three times yesterday by a man called Rogers, but escaped. Last night he sold his entire property, consisting of a second-hand tractor, an old fliv, one radio set and the good will in a house-moving business for $450. He then took the train north with a girl called Mildred Rogers of this place.

I inspected the tractor formerly owned by Mr. Suggs. No wonder we couldn't supply him with repairs for it. It is not one of our tractors. It has no name plate, but I was able to identify it as a 1920 Model, Steel Elephant Tractor, made by the S. E. Tractor Company of Indianapolis. I talked on the phone with Mrs. Joseph Banks, whose husband formerly owned the tractor. She says her husband sold the old Earthworm Tractor three years ago to a man in Dallas. Mr. Banks owned four or five different kinds of tractors. Mrs. Banks remembered he had once bought tractor parts from the Farmers' Friend Tractor Company.

In regard to your suggestion that Mr. Suggs might be persuaded to buy a new tractor, I think this is hardly possible. It is reported that before he left, Mr. Suggs stated that he and Miss Rogers would be married and would locate in Chicago. He was uncertain what business he would take up, but said very emphatically it would be nothing in any way connected with house-moving, or with tractors or any kind of machinery.

[THE END]

# INDEX TO AUTHORS

# INDEX TO STORIES